THE CORSAIR'S (

A pirate doesn't ask for permission - he takes.

When I see the delicate human female collared and enslaved by the smuggler I'm about to swindle, I do what any male would do.

I take her from him. It's what I do best, after all.

Now Fran's mine, and I'm never giving her up. On board my spaceship, she'll be safe. She'll wear my clothes, eat my food, and sleep in my bed. I'll keep her safe from a galaxy that wishes her harm.

But my sweet Fran wants nothing more than to return to Earth. How can I take her home when she holds my heart in her dainty, four-fingered hands?

This story stands completely alone and is only marginally connected to the Ice Planet Barbarians series and Prison Planet Barbarian. You do not need to read those books in order to follow this one.

THE CORSAIR'S CAPTIVE

A SCI-FI ALIEN ROMANCE

RUBY DIXON

RUBY DIXON

1

_____

KIVIAN

*S*ome jobs are a real pain in the keffing ass.

I kick my feet up on the control panel of my ship, *The Dancing Fool*, and ignore the look Sentorr shoots in my direction. I'm not going to break anything, and I ignore his fussiness. Even if I kicked the control panel in with my boots, he'd gripe less than if I scuffed it, so I learned to ignore him long ago. I can deal with his griping.

It's the one on the other end of the comm that's making me wish I could hang up.

"As I've said, the plans have changed," the kaskri Senator Bom Th'lek continues in a calm voice, as if he hasn't just upended all of my hard work to get to this point. "We now require twice the amount of lethiul crystal than originally specified. Things have escalated on our end. We are, of course, happy to pay."

I snort. Keffing right they'd be happy to pay. I rub a hand on my forehead, wishing I could perhaps jab a finger right through to my brain and put myself out of my misery. "You do realize we run a four-man crew here? It's not like I'm swimming in soldiers. Asking me to double the original payload changes everything. There's credits to be considered, and the meet-up itself, and—"

"I'm sure you'll find a way," Bom Th'lek tells me. "Just make it happen or we have no deal." He terminates the signal before I can.

I growl and slam my fist into the comm panel. "Three keffing weeks we've been working on this job, laying the groundwork to meet our contacts, and now he decides that he wants double?"

"It's almost like piracy doesn't pay," Alyvos says dryly.

"Quiet," I tell him, irritated. I've heard this same story from our nav over and over again. Ex-military are the biggest nags, but Alyvos knows what he's doing at least, and he's paid well to be a pirate. He's just a keffing hypocrite. I'm in a bad mood already; I don't want to hear more nagging from him.

"So what now?" Tarekh, our medic, asks. "Do we abandon the gig?" He leans against the port console, a frown on his big ugly face. "Expose 'em? Leak the intel to their government?"

I rub the shaved sides of my head, thinking. The kaskri are assholes, but they also pay well and they're repeat customers. They're not afraid to do shady things and pay well for them. If we sell them out, we get our five minutes of revenge, but we also lose a lot of credibility. A corsair that can't keep his mouth shut about a job is an unemployed corsair...or a dead one. "We'll go through with it," I tell my crew, musing on the changes. "It's still a good paying job we've put a lot of credits into, and a lot of time."

Sentorr gives me a curious look. "And then?"

"And then we'll charge them double if they actually want their cargo," I tell him with an easy smile, getting to my feet.

"Yes, but how are we going to do this? It took weeks to line up the meeting at Haal Ui Station as it is." Alyvos looks concerned.

"I'll figure it out. I just need to think on it for a bit and pick out my clothes." I glance over at Sentorr. "You have the bridge."

He snorts at my response but turns to face his controls, already back to work. That's why my men are so good at what they do. We can bicker, but when it comes down to the task, we all work together.

I stalk through my ship, heading to the captain's quarters. This isn't the first time we've had a hitch in a job, and it won't be the last. I just need to think things through. I trail my fingers along the wall as I move through my ship, lost in thought. Truth is, I'm not thinking much about the job and how much of a screw-up it's turning out to be. My thoughts are a million miles away. I don't see the scatter of tools stacked along a shelf near the hull, and I barely notice as I kick aside a canister of empty fuel processor to get to my room. I pass my hand in front of my panel lock, and the door to my suite opens. I close the door after me, and as I do, I close my eyes as gentle music begins to play. The rest of the ship may be a mess because Tarekh's in charge of cleaning and he's a slob, but in here, all is in order.

It helps me to think.

Jobs come and go. Kaskri are always trying to change jobs on us, which is one reason why they have to deal with pirates instead of regular merchants. Well, that and they're trying to buy illegal goods. That's not what's bothering me. It's something else.

I stare at the metal overhead compartment without seeing it. I need to focus on our destination—Haal Ui Station—and our problem: double the amount of lethiul crystal and how I'm supposed to get enough when I've only got the money for one load. Our contact at the station is as arrogant as he is idiotic, so it shouldn't be too hard to con him into double the cargo. I just need a sound plan.

I glance over at my closet. It's full of intricate, high-end weaves and custom-made fabrics. No synths for me. It's all part of the image I portray to others—that as a pirate, I'm a bit of an idiot who's more interested in shiny objects and fancy clothing than dirty work. It all started as a hook for a rather stupid client, and when it continued to work several jobs later, I added it to my permanent repertoire. No one fears a fancily dressed mesakkah male with immaculately styled hair, wearing the finest in fashion who pilots a ship with a silly name.

That's exactly what I want them to think. I want them to underestimate me. Of course, I haven't confessed to anyone that I've grown a particular fondness for the expertly made clothing and the way it shows off my form. Even I know when to keep my mouth shut.

I don't head to my closet, though. Instead, I pick up my portable communicator and tap through to the last message. It flashes the date received and then begins to play. My older brother's big grinning face appears on screen, and he hardly looks like himself. Growing up, Jutari was cool, almost cold. During his corsairing, he was competent and efficient, well-groomed and lethal. Even as a prisoner, he'd lost weight and acquired a hunted look on his face. He looked nothing like the sweaty, slightly dazed man that shows up on the comm.

"Chloe's pregnant," he says into the message, scrubbing at his brow and giving a wide-eyed shake of his head. "Frontier doctor finally got here and got her the shots she needed. Seemed to take right away. Of course, it might be because we made sure we used every opportunity for fertilization." He laughs, the sound pure delight. Somewhere behind him, a voice calls out and his face lights up. "That's her right now. Let me get her so she can tell you herself." The camera on the comm bobs and weaves and then there's a flash of a pale, sweaty human female leaning over the bed of what looks like Jutari's little farm out on Risda III. It's bumfuck in the middle of nowhere, but you'd never know it by the joy on my brother's face. The female—his mate—mumbles something and hides her face in a bowl. Before I can wonder about that strange movement, she makes a retching sound and Jutari turns the camera back on himself with a grimace. "Now's not a good time. Chloe's been a little sick ever since the doctor left, and it seems we know why." He grins, all teeth. "You're going to be an uncle. What do you think of that?"

I haven't sent my reply to my brother yet. I don't know how to tell him that I don't really care and he's probably going to make the keffing ugliest baby ever.

I'm still getting used to his strange-looking human mate. I can't imagine what a hybrid will look like.

My brother grins a dopey, contented smile at the camera. "At any rate, this isn't just to tell you our good news. We don't get many visitors out here, but if I can convince you to come and say hello the next time you're between jobs, you should swing by. Chloe would love the company. And she'd also love if you brought her some sweets. She's been getting cravings." He pauses. "Lots and lots of sweets. I'll give you the credits. But even if you can't get sweets for her, just come visit." He glances back up at the bed and then points a finger right at me, as if he can see me through the recorder. "That's an order, you sack of gollack shit. Come and say hello." The camera pans away for a moment as if Jutari's about to turn it off, only to blink back to him a moment later. "Oh, and

Chloe says she likes sour things too. So bring sweets and sours." He grins again, and then his face winks out, the message done.

My brother, the former assassin. My brother, once one of the most feared mercenaries in three galaxies. Now a farmer and soon to be a father. A grinning idiot mated to a very odd-looking human female who's now going to carry his even odder-looking baby.

It's...strange.

I didn't think anything of it when I rescued Jutari from the prison planet. He'd sent the signal, and I'd responded. My own "emergency" disk is still buried in the soft tissue of my cheek, and I can wiggle it with my tongue when I'm bored or thinking, kind of like now. I've never had occasion to use it. I can cut it from my cheek with a bite, remove the disk and then activate it and my brother would come for me, no matter what, no matter when. No questions asked. It's been a family tradition, much like piracy. My father was the one who had us implant the disks and with them, he imprinted into us the idea that if your brother is in trouble, you come for him.

I've never had need to use my disk, but Jutari did.

When I picked him up on the surface of the prison planet, I really hadn't expected him to bring a passenger, much less a female. Much less a *human* female, a species too primitive to be allowed to join the galactic community. Their planet's outlawed and the only humans I've ever seen are slaves on the black market. As a crew, *The Dancing Fool* won't touch jobs involving slavery or trafficking of any kind. Too messy. The closest I ever got to a human was when my brother showed up with one, announcing she was his.

I think of my fierce brother and the small, fragile human who seemed very out of her depth aboard the ship. She was quiet, sticking close to my brother's side, but brave enough, I suppose. I thought perhaps he was taking her with him out of gratitude or maybe as a pet.

It surprised me to hear he took her as his mate. Surprises me even more that they've had a babe together. And my brother—the infamous assassin—looks...content. Happy.

With a mate and a farm and a child on the way.

It's so very strange.

Perhaps those years in prison changed him more than I realized. Perhaps to him, an ugly female he owes a debt to deserves gratitude and his protection, and since they are both living on a remote planet, perhaps she started to look attractive to him.

Perhaps.

I think of the blissful expression on my fierce brother's face as he held his mate and the way he pressed his mouth to his mate's as if it were nothing. As if dozens of hygiene laws in every galaxy didn't exist to warn against that very thing.

I shudder.

Maybe all that time in prison made my brother a deviant.

Maybe that's why all of this bothers me and makes me restless and ill at ease.

A NAP SETTLES MY HEAD, and by the time I wake up, I've come up with a new plan. I change into fresh clothing, lacing my intricate sleeves, and head to the mess hall in the ship. Tarekh's there, shoveling noodles into his mouth, and Sentorr has a cup of tea in front of him.

"Well?" Sentorr asks. "Did you come up with a new plan?"

I nod, and we send a comm alert to Alyvos for him to join us. When our fourth enters the room, I begin to explain my changes. I feel good, more like myself. I like living on the edge, and I like a challenge. I like outwitting our enemies and proving just how much smarter we are by robbing them.

And I'm not going to think about my brother and his odd human mate, not while there are bigger problems.

I rub my hands together, ready to do this. Double the lethiul crystal means double the payload for us. The original plan had involved meeting our contact, Jth'Hnai. He's an ooli merchant, new to smuggling, and wants to meet at the bar on Haal Ui Station. Works for me. Public or not, I can do business either way, and Haal Ui is a sketchy sort of place on the edges of known space. I'll buy him a few drinks to be friendly, play the idiot pirate, pay him for his crystal...and then steal our credits back the moment he leaves the bar.

The plan hasn't changed too much in that regard.

I'm still going to buy the smuggler a few drinks, but I'm going to feel him out about the crystal and if he's got more. His response will tell me everything—if he gets greedy, then he has more with him. Cagey means he doesn't but he's got contacts. Angry means he doesn't have any more at all. So we'll see.

Gambling's the main part of the plan tonight. It's the oldest game in the book, but it's because it works so well on idiots. We'll play a few hands and I'll lose just to make him grow careless. Eventually we'll play for the crystal. If he *does* have more crystal, we get all of it. It might mean using a bit more muscle than originally planned, but we've got it under control. While I'm plying our ooli friend with drinks, Tarekh's going to station himself inside the bar, hiding in the crowd as silent backup if needed. Alyvos and

Sentorr will be on the station to transport the crystal from their docking bay to ours.

I'll be gambling and playing the fancy-clothed idiot pirate with our contact.

It's a fool-proof sort of plan, and Jth'Hnai won't suspect a thing. The ooli merchant's just now wetting his feet into the black market, and we're going to get in and make our fortunes before he wises up to the realities of working with pirates.

It should all go perfectly, providing everyone sticks to the plan.

2

FRAN

*Y*ou've never been groped until you've been tentacle-groped. There's no feeling of helpless violation quite like an alien shoving his feelers up your skirt and latching a sucker onto your ass.

It's not something I ever thought I'd feel, but I'm having a lot of firsts lately.

First time to ever wake up and find that I've been snatched from my bed? Check.

First time to ever see an alien? Check.

First time sold into slavery? Check. Check. Check.

The little voice inside my head—the one that states the obvious at the most annoying times—I've taken to calling Duh Fran. Because every time it speaks, I say "Duh, Fran" to myself.

Today, Duh Fran is saying *Well, you did say you wanted a year off after graduating college to have some adventure.*

Thanks, Duh Fran. Thanks a lot. The universe has a sick sense of humor, because this wasn't quite what I had in mind.

The tentacle slicks up my skirt again and I wriggle away. Or try to, anyhow. There's not a lot of room for walking with the crowd in the bar, and what with the fact that I've got a short leash going from the collar around my neck to my captor's hand. I tug at the cuffs on my wrists, twisting desperately to get free, but no one pays attention. No one pays any attention to me in this hellish version of an alien titty bar. The ones that do aren't ones I want attention from.

I thought things were bad when I woke up and found myself in a cage, stripped of my clothing, my dignity, and any idea of what was going on. Somehow, I'd been snatched from my bed and taken to outer space. It seemed so ridiculous that I didn't believe it at first. I was sure it was a drug of some kind that had been slipped into the water at my apartment building. Something. Anything. Because this just didn't make sense. But as the days wore on and I kept not waking up, I had to accept the fact that this horrific world wasn't a bad dream or a chemical reaction—it was my new reality.

I was caged like an animal. My water was something that looked laughably like the bottle that hooked onto my pet hamster's cage when I was a kid. My food was a crunchy bar of something tasteless that I got twice a day. Clothes? Nope. Shoes? Nope. Answers? Nope. I was treated like an animal, right down to some sort of weird absorbent plastic-ish sand in my cage that I suppose doubled as a toilet for all the "livestock." It was humiliating and awful, but I wasn't the only one kept captive. There were green beings and a bright red one, a creature that looked like a cross between an elephant and an armadillo, and another human female that I saw in passing. It was clear that I was going to be sold as a pet of some kind.

That cage was my home for a few days, I think. I didn't have a watch, but the lights on the ship—or space station, or wherever I was—cycled low from time to time, so I counted those as days. Two days in, some awful, bulb-shaped device was implanted in my ear that translates alien languages. Two days after that, I was taken from my cage, then washed and scrubbed by a creature that looked more sea anemone than human. It wasn't more than a few hours after that that someone arrived at my cage.

A buyer.

I barely pay attention to the alien staring at me from the other side of the metal grid. Aliens came and went all the time. Sometimes they fed me, sometimes they stared. None of them ever freed me, so it didn't matter.

"If you want her, she's yours," one of the zookeepers says, and that makes me pay attention. Two minutes later, I am given a wrap to wear around my thighs and a long, decorative necklace that bounces around my tits and hides nothing. I push my long hair forward to cover them—not that it does any good because a few minutes later, my new "owner" is back with a collar for my neck and cuffs for my wrists. I'm leashed and led out of my cage like a puppy in a pet store.

It's so...humiliating.

When he slides a hand under my skirt and squeezes my butt cheek, I slap his hands away. He only gives a weird croaking laugh and tugs on my collar, dragging me forward.

I'm pretty sure this guy's not looking for someone to do laundry, if the costume I've been given and the ass-grab are any indication. *Duh, Fran.*

The man that bought me jerks on the chain at my neck again. Okay, "man" might be a bit of a stretch. He looks more like a cross between a giant stuffed dinosaur and a bloated frog. His "hands" are stubby feelers tipped with suckers, and his gaping mouth is the most prominent feature he has. He's at least a foot taller than me, maybe more, and his girth is more "crushing" than petite. I'd wonder what the hell he wants with a human slave since I'm pretty sure our anatomy doesn't fit, but judging from the enormous codpiece he's sporting under that gut, "fitting" together isn't big on his priority list.

And then I'm shuddering because I'm picturing what's under that codpiece. God help me.

I've been fighting my terror for the last hour or so, but as the frog-man drags me out of the cage room and down a hall, I realize that there's no intention of treating me kindly.

I've been sold as an alien sex toy. I'm a trained poodle you can fuck. The thought is disgusting and beyond awful, and between moments of panic and outrage, I'm thinking of how to get out of this. There just has to be a way out. This can't be my life.

Every minute that passes, though, the horrors just get worse. He drags me from hall to hall and then out into a pod of some kind that bobs and weaves when we step onto it as if it's floating on water. The windows show nothing but stars and nebulae, and I get dizzy when the pod sways. Two other frog-men wait at control panels, their oddly beady eyes watching me in the creepiest of ways. I hug my arms over my torso, chilled to the bone despite the swampy, moist heat emanating from inside the ship.

What do I do now? I glance behind me at the gray metal corridor we just came down. Do I try to make a run for it? Hope someone at the space station will treat me better?

My owner jerks on my chain again, dragging me forward. I don't have a choice. I have to follow. Reluctantly, I get into the craft. Froggy straps himself into a seat and barks an order at his equally froggy men. He jerks on my chain again and points at the floor at his feet.

Is he serious? I'm supposed to kneel like a dog? I'm tempted to pee on his shoes like a misbehaving one.

He adjusts the straps on his chair and I glance around for mine. "Where do I sit?" I ask in English.

Froggy burbles something and points at his feet again. The translator makes it clear to me. That's my spot.

I open my mouth to protest, but then the ship-pod lurches downward and I'm knocked off my feet. I nearly choke on the chain itself and end up prostrate at my captor's feet anyhow. Gagging, rubbing my neck, I manage to sit up.

Froggy pats my head.

In a way, all the mistreatment's a good thing. I'm far too pissed to be frightened of rape. I know it's on the table. I know it's coming. But right now I'm just so damn angry at being treated like a bad dog that I can't think past that. No wonder dogs fucking run away from their owners. Right now all I can think of is escaping.

Sweat pools on my skin, making my hair stick to my neck and shoulders. It's humid as heck inside this ship, but I seem to be the only one uncomfortable. The others seem just dandy. I guess I should be glad I'm in little more than a diaper or I'd have heatstroke.

Except I'm not glad. I'd rather have the heatstroke.

The small pod-ship lurches on and Froggy leans forward in his nice comfy chair. "Vaashnaamh?"

I stare at him resentfully, waiting for the translator to kick in. It doesn't, though.

He points at his chest and burps up something that the translator doesn't get, and then points at me and repeats himself. "Vaaashnaamh?"

Oh, is he asking my name? How kind of him. "Fido," I snap back. "Arf fucking arf."

"Fhdo," he agrees, and then laughs as if this is the funniest thing he's ever heard. To his men, he calls, "Human language is so stupid. It sounds like they are vomiting."

He...does realize I'm wearing a translator and I can understand him? I glare resentfully at him, realizing this conversation isn't for me. His men just burp froggy laughter and talk about my anatomy in rather horrifying terms as the tiny ship floats through space.

I'm even more terrified when we dock, imagining a huge frightening bedroom and what the next chapter brings in this book of horrors. To my surprise, we descend from a ramp into...what looks like a bar or a club. And as my owner tugs on my chain, I realize he's bringing me along with him. Fucking hell. I tear feebly at my chains, but despite his froggy pudginess, my captor is strong and unrelenting.

As he drags me forward into the crowded club, I see all kinds of aliens of every awful shape and size, and shrink back as they reach out to touch my hair or flick at my skirt. Everyone's fascinated by the human. They coo with interest as some weird, shrill music plays in the background and a thick haze of scented smoke perfumes the air. Bodies of every shape and color gyrate on the floor, and small tables float in midair at the edges of the room. Aliens nibble on slidey-looking bubbles that pour from the lid of a small container in front of them. It's like a tripping bananas version of the cantina from *Star Wars*.

Into the fray, my alien owner drags me forward. Everyone seems fascinated by my appearance, and my owner puffs up with pride, telling them all about how much I cost. I relax a little. Maybe I *am* the intergalactic version of an exotic poodle and all he wants to do is show me off.

But then Froggy grabs my hand and pushes it onto his enormous codpiece and I realize that was a futile hope after all.

I'm definitely dying tonight, I realize. Because if this guy tries to rape me, I'm going to fight until the bitter end before I let him get under my skirt. I'm pretty sure that's exactly where he's planning to go.

Duh, Fran.

KIVIAN

My ooli contact's brought a slave with him.

A human slave.

I try not to stare as Jth'Hnai waddles up to the table, as ungraceful and ungainly as all of his people are on regular gravity space stations. I'm expecting to see him and his slimy face and gaping mouth. I've dealt with ooli before, and while they're not my favorites, I've seen stranger things.

I've prepared for this meeting for days. I've gone over the plan with my crew. Reloaded weapons, refueled the *Fool*, and even stashed extra weapons in lockers around the station. I've dressed in my fanciest trou and jacket, both made of the embroidered Sashim fabric that says I've got money and a foolish way of spending it. I have rings on several fingers and have re-capped my horns with engraved precious metal. I look like a dandy more than a pirate, and that's intended. I've dosed up on my antidotes just in case someone tries to poison my drink.

I'm prepared for this meeting.

Nothing's prepared me to see a human creature trailing behind my ooli contact, one that looks so much like Jutari's Chloe that I have to do a double-take. The ooli lumbers forward, moving to sit across from me at the table I've selected at the back of the bar. I know I shouldn't stare, but I can't help it. This is only the second human I've seen close up.

She's fascinating. For one, she's very bare. Clearly clothing her was not high on Jth'Hnai's list of priorities. The scraps she's been given to cover her body would violate laws on several planets, and others in the seedy club are staring. I don't blame them. Her skin is a creamy golden color a shade or two darker than Chloe's whitish-pink, and she's completely without scales or protective plating. She looks so...smooth. So dainty.

So touchable. My fingers practically itch to caress her.

Her hair looks soft and shiny and dark. Her breasts are surprisingly prominent under the decorative necklace she wears that is imprinted with the symbols of the ooli's clan. It jangles and bounces against them and draws the eye there. She's aware of it, too, judging by the way she pulls her hair forward over her breasts. Around her neck is a thick collar, with a lead attached to it.

"Do you see my pet?" Jth'Hnai rumbles at me. He leers at his slave and jerks on her chains, pulling her forward. "She's new. A fresh shipment just came in and I snatched her up before anyone else could get her. Cost me a pretty credit, too. You see what success can buy you, Kivian?"

"I do," I murmur, admiring. I know I shouldn't stare, but I can't help myself. She's completely foreign looking and yet hauntingly beautiful. Her features are delicate, her bones fragile, and yet there is an angry ferocity I never noticed in Chloe's eyes. My brother's mate seemed sweet and gentle to her core. This one spits fire from her eyes, and when Jth'Hnai pulls on her chains, she lets her expression tell him of her loathing.

I'm fascinated by her. I also know I can't let the ooli leave with her.

She's *mine.*

As a race, mesakkah are a possessive lot. We don't share well as a culture, and we're not good with understanding the concept of "open hearts," a term I've heard other species use. We're selfish when it comes to our females. We recognize our mates on sight most times, and when we decide that a female is *ours,* we pursue her with dogged determination that will result in death before we give up. Mesakkah mate for life and we're very, very possessive of a female once we do. It's not to say that most males haven't experienced bedsport with a female or another. But it's different when you recognize your mate. You know in that moment that your life has changed and you'll never want another female like you want her.

I feel that way right now.

This female is mine, not the ooli's.

Every time he rips at her chain, it takes everything I have not to reach across the table and wrap my hands around his bloated gullet. I know enough about him—and the seedy place we're visiting—to know that it's a bad idea to attack in public. That would draw attention to us, and I might as well paint a target on our backs at that point. The crowd here—armed to the teeth and as mercenary as I am—will turn on me in an instant and neither myself nor Jth'Hnai will make it out alive.

That would be death for my small, fragile human female.

I've got to play it cool, even though every bone in my body is screaming for me to free her, to grab the ooli by his slimy head and pound it into the nearest wall until he apologizes for even keffing *touching* her lovely skin. I slide my hands under the table and rub them on my fancy trou, feeling sweaty and uncomfortable. This rendezvous was just about lethiul crystal until he walked in with her.

Now I need to walk away with the female and double the crystal.

There's no other choice.

It's a good thing for Jth'Hnai that I'm used to charming the hide off of anything I run into, even an ooli fool. I'll get the female and the crystals, and by the time I'm done, he'll think it was all his idea. "I see you've brought company," I tell him, smiling and leaning forward so I seem like I'm only interested in a polite sort of way. "Fascinating. Who's your little friend?"

He grabs her chain again, jerking her forward, and the female makes a little choking noise, her hands going to the collar around her neck. I clench my hands on my belt, because the urge to murder Jth'Hnai is growing stronger by the moment.

"She's mine, you sneaky corsair, so don't get any ideas."

I force myself to raise my hands into the air and chuckle like it's no big deal. "No ideas. Just curious. It's not often you see a human female in these parts."

"That's because they're rare," the ooli brags. "Very rare. You have to know the right people and have enough credits to spend on such a luxury."

"And what do you plan on doing with such a luxury?" I can't help but ask.

"Whatever I wish," he says, and then laughs as if he's said the funniest thing ever.

The female just glares at him mutinously. She gives a feeble tug on the chain at her neck, but it's clear that the ooli, fat and rancid though he is, is far stronger than her. He should be careful with such a treasure. She should be cosseted and protected, not dragged into this nest of thieves and lowlifes and paraded about. Even now I see unsavory creatures from distant planets eyeing her with far too much interest. And why shouldn't they? She's barely covered, her skin exposed for all to stroke and pet.

And there are many, many males that pass by our table and reach out to caress her. She hates all of them, I can tell from the look on her face. I've never felt so proud and alternately so helpless in my life.

She's not going home with him. Not if I have to die to save her from such a fate.

"What's a creature like that run on the black market these days?" I ask lazily as I press a finger to the refreshment bubbler, making it seem as if I'm here just for drinks. I might have to buy the female from him if charm doesn't work.

"More than you'd make on a dozen shipments of crystal, corsair." He smirks at me.

"Now that sounds like bragging." I keep my tone light and direct one of the refreshment bubbles toward my mouth, then snatch it from the air with a click of my fangs. The female flinches back, surprised, and I want to reassure her that there's nothing to be afraid of. Instead, I am forced to ignore her. "Piracy pays very well, my good friend, as long as you know how to handle yourself."

"And I suppose you think you do?" The ooli is clearly skeptical.

I just laugh. "I get by." I make it a point not to look at the female. "So you are interested in slaves? I'm afraid that's a market that *The Dancing Fool's* never gotten into."

"Slaves are a difficult cargo, I imagine. Fragile things, especially' humans." He leans over and pinches the human's bare arm with his meaty fingers. "Look at this one. She's a little weak," Jth'Hnai croaks, then moves his head back and forth in the ooli version of a shrug, since they don't have shoulders. "But as long as her cunt is wet and tight, I don't care."

My jaw clenches. He's not getting anywhere *near* her cunt as long as I'm breathing.

The female jerks back. "I can hear you," she hisses in her crude language, and I realize for the first time that she's got a cheap translator attached to her ear. I thought it was just more ugly decorations.

It makes me unreasonably angry. Translator chips are low-cost and can be injected under the skin behind the ear. It's painless and just about every being that's ever been to a spaceport has one. A translator bulb like the one hanging from her small ear is the cheapest route, but painful and annoying for the wearer, and shows just how much "care" she's been given since she was taken. I have to force myself to concentrate on the refreshment bubbles floating near my side of the table or else I'm going to reach across and strangle Jth'Hnai after all.

You're here for crystal, I remind myself. *You can get the female, but it's going to cost you a small fortune if you don't get the crystal to boot.* A good pirate is always calm. My father said it often, and I always thought he was lecturing me. Maybe he was reminding himself all that time, considering that both my brother Jutari and I were handfuls.

I keep the impassive look on my face as the ooli stuffs his face with the refreshment bubbles and talks about how much money he has. How this idiot has managed to stay alive—and succeed—with such a loud mouth is surprising. Even others nearby are starting to pay attention, and that's making me tense. Time to steer the conversation, and the perfect moment arrives when a second refreshment table winds its way toward us, offering new treats for our consumption.

He immediately grabs both replenishment packs and begins to suck them both down, not offering either to his slave. It's difficult to watch her get ignored, but I force myself to keep wearing a smile. "A double?"

"It was a long journey," Jth'Hnai says between slurps. "And since you're paying, why not?"

"Why not indeed," I say smoothly, straightening the cuffs on my long-sleeved jacket. "Please feel free to help yourself to whatever you desire." My appetite is long gone, but I'm not surprised to see that he picks up a few more canisters of refreshments from the table before the mechanized table putters back to the bar. "Shall we get down to business, then? The crystal?"

"In a safe place," he tells me. "My credits?"

"Ready to be handed over at a moment's notice." I sit back in my chair, relaxing, and pat my pocket to indicate that I have his money. I have no such thing, of course, but he doesn't need to know that. I pretend to scan the crowd, but I'm looking for Tarekh. Sure enough, he's watching from afar, pretending to lurk on the edges of the throng gyrating near the center of the floor. He nods at me, acknowledging that he's aware and ready. I turn away, because there's no signal to give. Not yet. I tilt my head and consider Jth'Hnai. "Let's talk about...acquisitions."

I can't help but look over at the human female when I say that.

She's watching me, her dark eyes narrowed, a tiny furrow in her brow as if she's trying to figure me out. She's magnificent. My cock responds with a surge when she scowls in my direction. I love that. I love that she's still fierce, even when her life is in danger.

She's my kind of female.

"What kind of acquisitions?" Jth'Hnai asks, clearly bored. "I'm not interested in anything but credits."

Spoiled slab of filth. "Credits are exactly what I wanted to discuss," I tell him smoothly. I lean in, letting my body language tell him that I have something exciting and secretive to bring to him. "My buyers are interested in more crystal."

He slows in his eating and chews on one last refreshment bubble. "How much more?"

I shrug. I can't ask for the full amount. Not yet. I have to play it easy. So I grin and tilt my head. "How much have you got?"

The ooli considers me for a long moment and then pulls the female against his side, stroking her hair in a way that makes my gut boil with rage despite the relaxed smile on my face.

I'm glad she slaps at his hands, no more patient for his petting than I am. "Piece of shit, don't touch me," she mutters, and the words come through loud and clear in my translator. I pretend to study a refreshment bubble. It's either that or burst into laughter.

"I have more lethiul crystals," Jth'Hnai says after a time. "But it will cost."

I spread my hands wide. "You know I'm good for the credits."

"It will cost quite a bit more," he tells me, the look on his face shrewd.

"How much more?"

"Double."

"Double for double the crystals?" I give him a genial nod. "I can do that."

He shakes his head. "Double *per* crystal."

Keffing ooli. That's robbery and he knows it. I pretend to consider it, scratching my chin before giving a small shake of my head. "That's a little too rich for my blood." I act crestfallen. "Unless you'd...I don't know, play me for it?"

Jth'Hnai lights up. I knew he would. "Sticks?"

I scratch my brow and lie, "I don't know. I'm pretty bad at sticks."

Actually, I'm really keffing good. Really good. It's the gold standard for gamblers and cheaters everywhere. A good con man knows just how to twist his wrist to ensure that his sticks land just the right way to scoop up the other guy's points and still make it seem like an accident.

But the last time I met Jth'Hnai for a trade, we played sticks and I lost badly on purpose. You never know when you're going to need to hoodwink a ooli in the future, and I considered it an investment.

Besides, I wasn't playing with my own money last time anyhow.

I feign reluctance even as Jth'Hnai eagerly taps the entertainment button on the table and a box of game pieces appears from a hidden compartment. He gets out the set of ornately carved sticks and begins to deal them out on the table. "We shall play, you and

I. Perhaps you will win enough money from me to buy some extra crystals, hmm?"

I mock-groan. "I don't know..."

"Come, do not be hesitant," the ooli says, gleeful. He's expecting to clean up like last time, and I can see the greed shining in his beady eyes. "Play me. Let us see how fortune treats you this night."

"Maybe one hand," I agree reluctantly, secretly pleased this is all working out exactly as I intended.

3

KIVIAN

a few hours later, I shake my fist and then cast my sticks down on the table for what seems like the dozenth hand. "Kef! Another loss." I fake-moan and then rub my brow. "There goes my fuel money for the next run. My crew's going to murder me."

Jth'Hnai croaks with glee, scooping the pile of credits towards his chest. At his side, the slave has taken to sitting on the floor, pulling at the collar on her neck. She looks exhausted, her pale face strained. *Not too much longer*, I want to tell her.

"That's it for me," I tell him, making a great show of putting away my playing sticks. "I'm almost tapped out."

The ooli grabs my hand. "One more round. Perhaps your luck will turn, eh?"

I hesitate. "I'm not sure."

"One more," Jth'Hnai insists, and I give in, picking up my sticks once more.

Three hands later, he's not smiling. I've won two of the last three —giving him a token win just to make sure he doesn't realize that I'm snowing him. I've also recaptured enough money that he can't back out now. His betting has been foolishly high for the last few hands and he's starting to regret it. Good.

I win the next hand, though I make it close enough that he thinks he could have won it.

And then I win the next.

By now, the pile of credits in front of him is dwindling rapidly, and I can see the stress appearing on his face. I continue to play it easy. Too much feigning of surprise will set him off, but no reaction will as well. You have to know just how to handle a situation like this, and I've done such a thing a dozen times before. I know how to play my audience.

Others have gathered around the table, watching our increasingly high-stakes games with interest. Amongst the onlookers is my crewman, Tarekh, who's moved closer to the action.

I let my prey take the next hand, just to keep him hooked. When I win the hand after that, Jth'Hnai makes a sound of frustration, tapping the one lone credit he has left on the table. His betting's been ridiculous, which was what I wanted. I needed him to get comfortable and then bet wildly, expecting to clean me out of all my credits and then some. Instead, he's been more and more reckless in an effort to win his money back, and now he's flattened.

"Perhaps we should end it here," I say smoothly.

"One more hand," the ooli tells me, and flicks the remaining credit on the table towards me. "Gather your sticks."

"I'm not sure." I pretend to hesitate.

"Come, come. One more hand. I deserve a chance to win back my money." He flicks his fingers at me, indicating that we should begin.

I heave a sigh. "If you insist."

By the time the first round is played, he's ahead. We pause to bet, and I consider carefully before placing a very restrained amount of credits on the table.

"Bah, you can do better than that," Jth'Hnai says gleefully. "Bet more!"

"You don't have the credits, friend," I tell him in my gentlest voice. "I'd be a fool to bet more against what you're putting up."

"Then I'll put up something else." He gestures at our game with eager hands, sensing victory. "My jewels? My ship?"

This is the part where I'm supposed to tell him I want the rest of the lethiul crystals. I'll win, walk away with double and my money, and the job's done. It's what I've come here to do. That's the plan.

Instead, I find myself saying, "Why don't you bet that little human pet of yours?"

The girl turns and gives me the most stunning glare I've ever seen. She's alert now, and it takes effort not to smile at her outrage.

Of course, I'm sure if I turn around, Tarekh is going to be glaring at me, too. I just won't look. He'll just have to understand.

Jth'Hnai thinks for a moment and then nods. "All right. If you win, you get her in your bed."

The female human jerks violently at her chain, trying to free herself. "Are you fucking high? I'm not going into *your* bed or his! I'm not anyone's property!"

He reaches over and swats her across the face. "Cease your whining!"

She staggers and drops to her knees, pressing her hand to her face. I can see a hint of bright red blood in her mouth.

I jump to my feet, the urge to protect her overwhelming. I'm going to kill this keffing bastard if he touches her again.

Jth'Hnai gives me a suspicious look. "What?"

I grit my teeth and lean in, forcing myself to be casual. "Not much of a prize if she's all wrecked, is she?"

He grunts. "Just play."

I don't look at the female. If I do, I'm going to get furious once more. I toy with the over-decorated cuffs of my jacket and then sit down once more, feigning a calm I don't feel. I'm raging inside. He *hurt* her and I have to sit here and pretend like it doesn't matter. Death from a thousand poisoned bubbles is too good for this ooli. Maybe a thousand poisoned pinpricks. That might be better.

I content myself with bloodthirsty thoughts of Jth'Hnai's death and it calms me. Just a little. Just enough that I can play my hand with steady confidence. My colors line up perfectly, giving me the score for that round. Jth'Hnai plays again, but I keep the advantage, and by the time we're out of sticks, I've trounced him solidly. I knew I would. There was no doubt in my mind. I've played sticks since I was a child and my father taught me all the best ways to cheat without being noticed...which I've employed tonight.

Jth'Hnai's face swells with anger. "You...you cheated."

"No, I didn't."

I did. But he doesn't need to know that.

I lean forward and grab the links of the chain that leads to the female's throat. "I'll be taking my prize home with me now."

He slams his slimy hand down over mine before I can lift her chain. "I didn't say you could keep her. I said you could have her in your bed. You only get one night."

I narrow my eyes at him, trying to recall exactly what he said. "Just one night?" I echo. "I'm pretty sure I didn't agree to that."

"I don't care what you agreed to. If you want extra crystal—at any price—you'll abide by the rules." His face is turning a darker shade of green, indicating his rage.

Hmm. I consider for a moment. Walk away with the female now and lose all the crystal? Or play along for a little longer? I suppose I can continue the game for a while yet. I wink at Jth'H-nai. "I'll warm her up for you, then."

The female makes an outraged sound.

FRAN

I've been traded. Is there no end to tonight's indignities?

Granted, if I have to fuck an alien, I'd rather it be this one than the frog.

Duh, Fran.

I don't want to sleep with *anyone*, of course, but I'm having a hard time remaining outraged when the big blue brute is so... well...*dang.* He's kind of amazing looking. Sure, he's blue and has an enormous set of metal-covered curling horns that make his head look gargantuan. He's wearing some ornate clothing with blowsy sleeves that can't quite hide the fact that the breadth of his shoulders is staggeringly huge, and he's got thick black hair cropped short and shaved on the sides of his head, laughing dark eyes, and a mouth that looks like a dream.

Too bad he's such a dickhole.

I can't believe the guy just bargained to have a night with me. It doesn't matter how good he looks. These aliens just bet me at a table as if I'm nothing. Any sort of attraction I might have felt for the guy died in an instant at that. I'm not human to him, just like to Froggy. I'm a plaything surrounded by a lot of much bigger aliens, and it sucks. I close my eyes again, hoping desperately that I'm going to wake up from this unending nightmare.

All I get is another jerk on my neck-chain that makes me gag. Froggy tugs on it one last time, releasing me to the blue guy's care. "She's yours...for now."

"Wonderful." The grin on his face is downright roguish—and displays long sharp canines I never noticed before. He takes my chain and gives Froggy an elegant bow. "I'll return her to you in one piece."

Prince Charming he's not.

"Oh, I didn't say I was leaving," Froggy tells him as he starts to walk away. "I'm going to watch."

Well, this just gets worse and worse. I tug on the chain, trying to break free...not that there's any place to go. I just know I don't want to go anywhere with these two.

"Going to watch, are you?" the big blue one says with a laugh. "I'm not sure if I'm a fan of having my technique criticized." He gives a wave, indicating I should follow him, and when I don't, he sighs and grabs my waist.

The next thing I know, I'm slung over his shoulder like a sack of potatoes, my ass in the air.

"Put me down, you bastard!" I slam a fist against his back and then wince, shaking my wounded hand back and forth. Is he wearing armor under his clothes? Because I think I just busted my knuckles.

"Calm yourself, little one," the big blue alien says, and pats my butt in a rather humiliating show. "Now, Jth'Hnai, I don't think I'm a fan of you inviting yourself to our little party. I won fair and square—"

"She's expensive," Froggy says bluntly. "I'm going to make sure you handle my property correctly."

"Your property is going to be so well 'handled' that you're going to have a hard time pleasing her once I'm done," he teases.

I snort and rub my wounded knuckles. "Fucking unlikely."

The blue alien just chuckles. Seems he's overheard me. He pats my ass again, and then we start bobbing away through the crowd.

I close my eyes, waiting for all of this nightmare to pass. Hands— or tentacles—grab and touch my bare legs as we cut through the crowd, just like they've been touching me all night. I shiver when something particularly slimy brushes my bare foot. Is this what my life's going to be like from now on? An endless stream of strangers grabbing me and using me? Despair fills me at the realization.

The big alien carrying me pauses. His shoulder jerks, and the crowd gasps. "Did you just touch my female?" he growls at someone nearby.

"I didn't mean it!" an alien stammers, just out of my line of sight.

"Really? Because I thought I just saw you touch her leg. Should we ask her?" He sounds ferocious, and he sounds pissed.

He's...defending me? I'm shocked.

"No, no," babbles the stranger. "I promise I won't do it again. Don't hurt me!"

"If you didn't do it, how can you do it again?" Big Blue says, and there's so much menace in his voice that I shiver. I don't know what to make of this.

There's a soft thump, and then the crowd around us seems to breathe a sigh of relief.

"Anyone else want to touch my female?" Big Blue dares the crowd.

It's silent.

"Yours only for tonight," Froggy chimes in, and I want to slap him.

"Mm," is all that Big Blue says. Then he starts walking again, the hand returning to my butt once more.

This time I don't kick. I'm not a fan of the ass-grab, but if it saves me from having tentacles sliding up my skirt, I'll deal with one hand instead of eighteen. His defense of me was...downright menacing. I shiver.

The music fades and I sway back and forth on the alien's shoulder as he moves down a long, gray corridor. The one holding me keeps up casual chatter with Froggy, talking about how the station's changed since the last time he came through, and how he's surprised at his luck at the game they played, and how he hopes Froggy doesn't have any hard feelings. A long, blue tail sways behind him as he walks.

Froggy's pretty silent despite this upbeat one-sided conversation, which tells me he probably does have hard feelings. Lots of them.

Good. Fuck him. Fuck them both.

We go down another hallway, and Froggy makes a noise that sounds like a protest. "Where are we going?"

"Why, back to my ship, of course," Big Blue says cheerfully. "That's where my bed is. Though I do admit you're probably going to find it cramped. I normally don't entertain in threes, you know."

"No," Froggy says. "If you take her on your ship, I'll never see her again."

"So mistrusting. I'm hurt," Big Blue says playfully.

"You're a pirate," Froggy points out. "I'd be a fool to think otherwise."

Big Blue only laughs, and his tail flicks back and forth.

"I have a room," Froggy says, and pushes ahead. "Follow me."

"If you insist, though I promise I'd treat her well if you gave us some privacy." He caresses my backside with one of his enormous hands.

I make a sound of protest and slam my manacled fists against his armored back. "Dick."

That earns me a second pat on the ass.

We turn down hall after hall, sometimes passing other inhabitants of the space station. Occasionally someone will exclaim surprise at the sight of me, and it makes my stomach sink. If they're so startled to see a human, does that mean my chances of ever getting home are nonexistent? I don't know if it's a good thing or a bad thing that I'm so unfamiliar. I don't like the thought of a bunch of other slaves wandering around…but I like the thought of being the only one even less. That means I can't count on anyone or anything to help me.

"Wow, you're really in the bowels of the station here, aren't ya, Jth'Hnai?" the alien holding me comments. I realize a moment later that the tangle of sounds must be Froggy's name. I can't pronounce it. "Can you even contact your ship from this pit?"

"I prefer my privacy," Froggy of the unpronounceable name says.

"So do I. Which is why you should leave me alone with your little pet here," Big Blue replies.

The guy just does not give up.

Froggy grunts some sort of response, and then I hear a soft hiss, and the pressure change makes my ears pop. A door must have opened. "Inside."

"What, with you and your guards? Gonna be mighty crowded in that bed." The big blue guy seems unconcerned despite his words.

Guards too? I look up and catch a glimpse of some froggy-looking legs behind us. There's at least two more in the hall a few steps behind the alien carrying me.

An orgy? Great. I didn't think my life could get any worse, but I guess I'm wrong on all counts.

Duh, Fran.

I…feel like crying. I know I should fight, but the terror and exhaustion of the last few days have taken my last few ounces of strength. Hot tears slide down my face and drip onto the floor as Big Blue enters the room and carries me forward. I sniffle, trying to be quiet—and then I realize that it doesn't matter. They don't care if I cry either way.

So I let myself cry. I've been strong for days and it's gotten me nowhere. I might as well give in to the tears and despair that are tearing me apart inside.

No sooner do I let out a sob than I'm flung backwards onto something soft. A bed. I bounce, startled, and look up to see the big blue alien looming over me. His eyes narrow at the sight of me, and then he puts his hands to his belt, glancing over at Froggy who lurks nearby. "I can't talk you out of leaving? Little Kivian here's a bit shy with an audience." He gestures at his crotch.

"Little" might be a misnomer. It looks like he's packing serious heat there, and that makes me sob again, drawing my knees tight together.

"Not leaving," Froggy tells him.

Big Blue sighs. "Very well, then." He taps something on his belt, then gets on the bed and crawls forward on hands and knees toward me.

Alarmed, I try to skid backwards, only to collapse underneath him just as he covers me.

He leans in and presses his cheek to mine. "Stall," he whispers, and then sits up, pretending to study me.

Stall? Did I hear him right? Did my translator interpret that correctly? I blink up at him, surprised.

He touches the necklace between my naked breasts, and I automatically grab his wrist to stop him. His eyes widen, and he grins at me, as if delighted at my resistance. Big Blue leans in. "What's your name?"

"Her name is Fhdo," Froggy says.

I don't know whether to laugh or scream in frustration. When the blue alien looks at me, waiting, I slap at his hand again. "Fuck you."

"Strange name," he murmurs. "I'm Kivian."

"I don't care," I hiss at him.

"So unfriendly. I guess I deserve that." He leans down over me again, planting one big hand on each side of my head. "Though it's going to make things a little difficult in a few minutes."

I narrow my eyes at him. "Because you're going to rape me?"

His mouth twists as if in distaste. "Wouldn't call it rape."

"Why? You think I'm going to enjoy it?" I give him a look that tells him just what I think of that idea.

The big blue—Kivian—just chuckles. "Didn't say that, either." His hand moves and he caresses my bare arm, thoughtful. "You're so soft."

I jerk away from him. "And you're such a creepy prick. Oh, wait, is this the part where I hand out grateful blowjobs because I'm so happy you're not beating me to death? Go fuck yourself."

His grin widens, displaying those sharp, white teeth. "You've got quite the mouth on you. I like that."

"Are you going to talk her to death or are you going to fuck her, Kivian?" Froggy demands.

"This is part of my foreplay," Kivian calls out. "I'm getting her in the mood."

"No, you're not," I retort.

Kivian puts a finger to his smiling lips in the universal gesture for silence. He acts like all of this is a big joke. What the hell's wrong with him? "If you keep being mean, I won't be able to get into the proper mood," he reminds me, almost chiding. He widens his eyes imperceptibly at me and then flicks his gaze over to the side, as if trying to communicate something quietly with me.

What is it? What is he talking about? Is this part of his "stall" thing? Or is that just another tactic to catch me off guard? I don't trust him. At all. Nervous, I skitter backward a bit more.

He grabs me by my leg, a wide grin on his face once more, and hauls my ankle into the air. "I must admit, the struggling is a novelty of sorts," Kivian continues, examining my foot. "Most females are practically flinging themselves at me every time I come into port. Hm. Five toes. Interesting."

"You're not down here to count her toes, you idiot," Froggy snarls at him.

I jerk my leg, trying to get free, but he's holding fast. Instead of letting me go, he runs the pad of his thumb down the sole of my foot, and it's surprisingly ticklish. Anger, loathing, and something else far hotter all skitter through me at once, leaving me confused.

"I don't see why I can't count her toes. They're utterly adorable." Kivian rubs his thumb over the bottom of my foot again and then leans in. "So small and pink and as soft as the rest of her." He hesitates and then glances over at Froggy. "Don't suppose you have any plas-film on you? Hygiene laws, you know."

Froggy snorts. "You mesakkah and your strange laws. We ooli do not care about such things."

"So you don't." Big Blue shrugs. "I suppose since I'm your guest, I must follow your rules." He runs a hand down his chest and undoes a few intricate knots that tie the fabric of his shirt together in the crazy, decorative fastenings. "Though I have to admit it'd be my first with skin to skin." His gaze flicks back to me, and another teasing smile curls his mouth. "You'll be gentle with me, won't you?"

"Fuck off," I say flatly, and kick at the hand holding my foot.

"I'll take that as a 'yes' despite your tone," he tells me, all cheerfulness. "Give me a wet cloth to wipe her down, my good friend." He extends a hand out to Froggy as if the alien's supposed to wait on him.

To my surprise, he does. "Don't see what this is for," Froggy grumbles in his weird language.

"Well, I plan on tasting her, but you haven't been taking very good care of the poor thing, now, have you?" He turns my foot ever so slightly and shows my dirty sole to both of us. "Look at how filthy she is." He tsks. "And here you say my people are strange for plas-film."

I gasp in surprise when the warm cloth touches my foot, bathing it. It's ticklish to feel him caress my skin with the damp material, washing it clean even as Froggy wanders away a few steps. I try to kick Big Blue's hands again, but he catches my other foot easily and moves to cleaning it. His big hand strokes up and down my calf, as if he's caressing me.

It almost feels good. Almost.

I really don't understand what's going on. This frightening, large alien with blue skin and the horns of a devil acts like he's prim and proper. Even his clothing is far more intricate and detailed than anyone else's I've seen. But the person that slung me over his shoulder wasn't a pampered lord of some kind. I felt muscles. Hell, I see them even now, bulging through the gossamer fabric of his shirtsleeves and covered in rough-looking tattoos.

It doesn't make sense. None of this does, right down to the incredibly intensive foot bath I'm getting. Is this part of his "stalling"?

I really don't understand what's going on.

"There. All better." Big Blue finishes washing my feet and tosses the cloth aside. He leans in and nibbles on my toes, lips teasing at my skin. I'm so startled at this that I can't do more than lie back and gasp. My body responds, however. Maybe it's the ticklishness of it or fear, but I can feel my nipples growing hard and my breasts tightening. It's the last thing I want—to feel any sort of attraction to this alien, no matter how forced.

I close my eyes and shake my head, trying to jerk my foot away from him. "Stop touching me."

"Where's the fun in that?" he murmurs around my toes. His tongue flicks against my skin again, sending shivers all through me.

I know this is leading to rape. *Duh, Fran.* I know this is awful and there's a detached part of my mind that's freaking out quietly. But I'm having a hard time focusing on that, because I can't stop staring as Big Blue's firm lips play against my skin. They're a slightly darker blue than the rest of him, and when his teeth flash, they seem incredibly white against his skin. It's oddly enticing, and I find myself waiting for another flash of those fascinating teeth and then the ticklish drag of his tongue against my foot. I can't pull away. All I can do is watch in mute horror-mixed-with-fascination as heat pools in my belly.

"Just stick your cock in her already and give me back my toy," Froggy says, and he sounds like he's pouting.

"Maybe we should ask FuckYou what she thinks of that idea," Kivian replies, and gives me a curious look. "Well? Or do you prefer Fhdo?"

I try to jerk my foot out of his grasp again. "I prefer neither." My pulse is pounding hard, and I hate that I can feel it especially hard between my thighs.

"Mmm. Well, I suppose I can stop asking, then. I guess the name doesn't matter after all." He holds my foot in one firm hand and caresses the arch of it, then rubs his lips over my ankle. "I do have to admit," he murmurs. "This skin-on-skin contact is positively decadent. No wonder there are so many lawbreakers out there." He trails his mouth higher, sliding his big body closer to mine as he moves down my leg.

I'm breathing hard, both frightened and—I hate to admit it—titillated at the same time. He rubs his mouth—it's not quite a kiss, not quite—along the back of my calf and then moves toward my knee...and my inner thigh. "So very many laws being broken," he says in a languid voice. "Can't say I'm displeased about that. I might become a hedonist after all. What do you think of that?"

His tongue flicks against the inside of my thigh.

I suck in a breath and my hands go to the front of my skirt, pushing the material down over my pussy protectively. I can just guess where he's heading, and I'm freaking out.

A little turned on, sure. *Duh, Fran.* But still freaking out.

Big Blue licks the inside of my leg again and then gives me a heavy-lidded look, his face framed by my parted thighs. "Did all the fight in you disappear, little one?"

I scowl at him, any pulsings of heat disappearing at that. "If you're asking if I want you to rape me, the answer is no. The answer will *always* be no."

"Didn't say it'd be rape," Big Blue repeats with an enigmatic smile.

Something gives a soft chime, and the big blue alien grins against my thigh.

"In fact, it'd be more like a rescue," Kivian murmurs.

I'm left trying to figure out what the heck that means. Before I can open my mouth to ask, Froggy waddles forward. "What's that noise?"

"That noise," Kivian says with a flourish, sitting up. "Is my crew contacting me. It goes off when it's time for me to go."

"Time to what—?" My owner's words are interrupted as Kivian pulls out what looks like a gun of some kind from the inside of his vest and aims it at Froggy's beady little eyes.

"Time. To. Go." Kivian says simply. "By now, my men have loaded your crystal onto our ship. So we'll be taking that. And we'll be keeping our money, too. Which is kind of neither here nor there since I won it all from you." He grins and then reaches down and gently takes my neck chain, twisting it around his hand. "I'll be taking this little one from you, as well. Come, my sweet FuckYou. Time to leave."

I stare at him uneasily, wondering if this is a joke. When he doesn't break into laughter or tell me that he's teasing, I glance over at Froggy. He looks furious, his gaze focused on the gun pointed at his head.

This...must be what he meant by *stall*.

He's rescuing me.

4

KIVIAN

*I*t's good for me that Jth'Hnai pays his guards so cheaply. If they were decent mercenaries, they'd have already disarmed me and splattered my brains all over the gaudy carpets of the room. As it is, they're just looking to their boss for direction, and he's not giving them any.

Works for me.

I give another gentle tug to the human female's chains, doing my best not to harm her. "Go and open the door, little one." I keep my gaze focused on Jth'Hnai, because I don't trust him not to worm his way out of this. He didn't get to be a rich ooli by playing by the rules, after all. "Do me a favor and have your men move to your side," I tell the idiot I'm robbing. "So I can watch all of you."

Jth'Hnai scowls at me and then flicks a hand at his men, indicating that they should join him. Just as I suspected. Cheap labor. It makes things so very easy it's practically criminal.

Oh wait. It *is* criminal. Oh well.

I wait patiently for the men to get next to their leader, and then I toss cuffs at the first one. "You know what to do."

He doesn't seem all that concerned, cuffing his buddy and then his employer before slapping the final pair on his own wrists and waiting for them to auto-link.

I give my blaster a little circle. "Now turn around, facing the wall." When they do, I look over at my female, who's watching me with narrowed eyes. She still hasn't moved from the bed. "Come, little one," I entice her. "We're going to have a hard time escaping with their loot if you don't start the getaway."

She looks surprised, then scoots to the edge of the bed and gets to her feet. "You're...taking me with you?"

Jth'Hnai makes an angry sound, but I ignore him. He no longer matters. "I'm afraid no one's going anywhere very fast if you don't open that door, my sweet." I gesture at the entrance to the room, still locked and still preventing my crew from entering.

The female nods slowly, dark eyes wide. "And you won't leave me here?" She glances over at the ooli. "With them?"

"I'd sooner shoot myself in the groin."

Jth'Hnai snarls. "Save that pleasure for me." He doesn't turn around, though. Coward. He's all talk and nothing more, just like I figured.

My little human gives me one last wary look and then moves to the door of the apartment. She studies the panel and then looks at me helplessly. I have to coach her through how to input the sequence to open it, but a moment later the doors open and both Sentorr and Tarekh enter, armed with their own weapons. The female skitters back a foot or two, casting an uncertain look in my direction.

"About time," I chide Tarekh and Sentorr. "Where's Alyvos?"

"With the ship." Tarekh tells me. They muscle in, casting a brief look at the female. "What's with the change in plans?" the medic asks, clearly in a bad mood. "We've been waiting on your ass for a good ten minutes to get back to the dock."

"I was busy wooing my female. Is everything loaded?" I avoid answering his question and move forward, nudging the ooli and his guards into the water closet. Jth'Hnai doesn't seem all that eager to go inside, but once Tarekh's massive bulk—massive even for a mesakkah—looms over them, they march inside without complaint.

We strip them of any sort of communicators, look for weapons, and then lock them into the water closet. Tarekh shoots a blast into the control panel, locking the door and preventing them from coming out for quite some time.

I turn to see that Sentorr has the neck chain of my little human female, holding her hostage once more. Her arms are crossed over her breasts, and she shivers, looking worried and scared, her face pale. "What do you want to do with this one?"

For some reason, the sight of him holding her chain fills me with an irrational flash of jealousy. Fighting the possessiveness surging through me, I force myself to walk calmly to her side and take the chain from him. He doesn't know that she's mine, so there's no need to grab him by the throat and choke the life out of him. "I'm taking all of Jth'Hnai's wealth," I tell the others. "And that includes her."

Tarekh makes a frustrated sound as he rejoins us. "What are we going to do with a thing like that? They're illegal."

"So is stealing crystal, but I didn't hear anyone complaining about that," I tell them lightly, and then touch my fingertips to the human's delicate chin. "Look up, please."

She scowls at me but does as she's told, and I attach an override key to her collar. A moment later, it falls from her neck, revealing the stark bruises that have been left behind. I make a low growl in my throat at the sight, and the urge to go back into the water closet and blast Jth'Hnai's slimy head off grows. Instead, I toss the chain to the floor. "You're free."

The human blinks at me in surprise, and she doesn't move when I do the same for her wrist-cuffs. Even after the metal clanks to the ground, she rubs her wrists and just watches me.

"Do you want to come with us?" I ask her.

Sentorr makes a noise of protest. I know what he wants to say. We're wasting time.

I ignore him, focusing on her.

She just gazes at the water closet, where Jth'Hnai and his men are trapped, then glances back at me. "What are my options?"

"Time to go," Tarekh says impatiently.

I pay no attention. He can wait a moment. She's more important. "You can stay here," I answer her. "But not many will help you. Even if I gave you clothing and money, a human is considered contraband. Others would immediately try to take you for their own and you might end up with a worse master than before."

"Will you take me back home?" she asks. "To Earth?"

"If I tell you the truth, little one, I must say no." It pains me to tell her the truth, but even my innocuous ship cannot get anywhere near that star system without risk.

She sighs. "Well, at least you're honest. All right, I'm coming with you." She points a finger at me. "No rape."

I'm amused at how she's making demands, despite the fact that she's clearly not the one in power in this situation. Fierce little one. I love that. "If I wanted to rape you, my sweet, would I have not done so already?"

"Not if your little Kivian doesn't like a show," she retorts.

I burst into laughter. So she caught that, did she?

Sentorr just gestures at the door. "If we're all done here, can we please go before the station security is alerted to our actions?"

I nod and put a hand on the human's back. "Come. Stay close to me."

She automatically moves closer, and her hand goes to my belt, as if she needs to latch on out of fear of being left behind. It fills me with a near-unholy sense of pleasure.

"Is that your name?" she whispers a moment later. "Kivian?"

"Sav Kivian Bakhtavis," I tell her with a playful grin. "At your service. And now, it's time for us to go."

FRAN

The unreality of the situation keeps growing. I keep expecting to wake up and find this all to be a dream. Or only half a dream, and I'll wake back up in the cage with someone throwing "human feed" at me like I'm a pet chicken.

Instead of being the slave of frog-men, I'm...free? I think.

And instead of being surrounded by frog-men, I'm with big blue guys with horns that look a bit like I imagine the devil might look if he decided to be a space alien.

It's all so bizarre.

"This is *The Dancing Fool*," Kivian tells me as he leads me out of the narrow passageway and onto the dimly lit deck of what must be his ship. There's dark metal and lit-up components everywhere, and all of it looks smooth and important and I'm afraid to touch anything. "She's my ship, and she'll be your home for the next while."

"*Dancing Fool*, huh?" I rub my arms and hug them, because not only is it a little chilly and I'm wearing less than a diaper, but it helps keep my tits covered. "Doesn't sound very pirate-y."

"And that is exactly the point," Kivian replies with an irrepressible grin. He immediately starts to strip off the layers of his ornately embellished clothing, like any man that's just been given reprieve from going to a fancy dress party. "No one is going to stop a ship called something so ridiculous and assume they're up to nefarious deeds."

The other two aliens busy themselves removing their guns and then move past us, heading down the hall.

"Come," Kivian tells me after he loosens the tight fabric at his neck and removes a layer of clothing. "Let's get to the bridge so we can get out of here."

"Wait," I tell him as he moves past me. "Can I have a shirt? Or something I can wear to cover up?"

He turns to me and rubs his jaw. "Of course. I don't suppose you run around in little more than a scarf on your home world, do you? I've heard humans are primitive, but I imagine that's a bit more than primitive."

"Yeah, sorry, I must have left my stone tools at home back in my cave," I tell him sarcastically. "Can I have a shirt or not?"

Kivian watches me for a long moment, and my skin prickles. Maybe I'm being too lippy with him and he's going to punish me. A slow grin spreads across his face, and then he shakes his head. "It seems I'm good at charming everyone but you." He opens his shirt, undoing complicated fastenings with the blink of an eye, and then shrugs it off.

My body prickles with alarm, wondering if this is when the rape happens. I step back warily, but he only holds the shirt out to me. Oh.

"I'm not going to touch you without your permission," he says in that calm, smooth voice. "When I said you were safe with me, I meant it. I won't harm you, and neither will my crew."

I study his face, wondering if this is a trick. If he's fooling me like he fooled the frog-guys. But I see nothing but calm confidence in his expression. It takes me a moment to realize his words aren't being filtered in through the ear piece. "You...you speak English?" I take the shirt from him and wrap it around my body, shoving my arms through the sleeves. It's like wearing a blanket because he's so large compared to most human guys, but I don't mind. It's warm and it covers everything, and that's all that counts.

Kivian moves forward, all bare skin. I notice for the first time that he's got a few old scars on his chest, white against the blue hue of his skin. Along one arm, dark black tattoos dance up his muscles in fascinatingly foreign patterns. He's impressively built, and not just because he's seven feet tall. It's clear he works out. It's also clear that the "armor" I thought I felt under his clothes was actually on his skin. He has hard ridges along shoulder and arm and across the center of his chest. He reaches for the front of the shirt and begins to move his fingers along the complicated knotwork of the ties, doing them up for me like I'm a child. Three fingers and a thumb, I notice. Just another bit of alienness.

Funny, because he's the first guy that's treated me like a person since I woke up a slave.

"I had my chip download your language the moment I saw you," he says. "Thought it might be easier to communicate."

"Chip?"

He taps one big finger against the back of his ear. "Language implant. They're common these days, just like anti-virus implants and the like. Yours is...cheap. Effective but cheap and uncomfortable."

I touch my ear, where the big bulb rubs against my skin. He's not wrong.

"Come," he says, finishing the ties on my shirt. "Time to go to the bridge before the others wonder if I've dragged you to my bunk." Kivian gives me another flirty, easy grin and then turns, heading down the hall after the others and treating me to a show of upper-back plating, lower-back dimples, and a swish of his tail.

All right, then. I can go and find a shadowy spot to hide like a coward, or I can suck it up and go hang out on the bridge. Much as I want to hide—or sleep, sleep would be nice—I force myself to follow him down the passageway. His shirt's so big that it brushes against my knees and the sleeves bury my hands. I shove them up my arms and then roll them up as I walk, trying to absorb everything about where I'm at.

I hate to say it, but the entire thing looks like it could have come out of a *Star Trek* episode or a space movie. I wonder if that's coincidence, or if someone in Hollywood's been visited by aliens himself. There are all kinds of panels on the walls—some dim and blank, some lit up with graphs and images and lights. There's something that looks like a keyboard with a lot fewer keys, and Kivian moves his hand over it—not touching it

—to open a door. The floor underneath my feet is cool and feels like ridged metal, and as we go inside the bridge of the ship, I see several workstations with big chairs, all of them occupied except the central one that clearly must belong to Kivian.

One of the big blue aliens turns and glares at us. His head is shaven, making his horns seem almost as prominent as the hawkish nose on his face. "About time." His gaze flicks to me. "It's bad luck to have pets on a ship, Bakhtavis."

"She's not a pet," Kivian says easily. "She's our guest." He puts his hand on my shoulder and leads me forward. "Come sit in my chair. You can belt in so you're safe on take-off."

Well, that's a welcome change from how Froggy treated me. I perch on the edge of his chair, feeling dwarfed by its great size. "What about you?"

He shrugs his big shoulders, moving forward to tap a button that makes straps spit out and conform to my body. "Do me good to get pitched around now and then."

"So, wait. We're keeping the human?" The shaved-head one frowns in my direction. "I thought we were just going after lethiul crystal?"

"Kivian found something else he wanted," the biggest of the aliens says.

Someone groans.

"All of you, silence." Kivian doesn't sound irritated but amused. "Just tell me if you were able to swing the crystal while I was busy distracting our ooli friends."

"Got the shipment...and a bit more, but not too much more. It's not all that the kaskri asked for," says one of the men.

"It'll have to do. We're leaving." Kivian grins at me and grips the arm of the chair. "Hold on tight, little one."

Hold on? Why?

"Surging," one of the aliens says, and that's the only warning I get before we shoot forward like a slingshot into outer space.

5

KIVIAN

The fragile human closes her eyes and rests in my captain's chair. She's dwarfed in my shirt, her strange soft skin covered from chin to knee.

I want to hold her close and protect her, but I know she wouldn't welcome it. I have to clench my hands to keep from reaching out and caressing her rounded cheek. Soon enough, she'll welcome my touches. I've never been spurned by a female I chased...not that I've ever chased particularly hard. I've always preferred a life of no encumbrances—romantic or otherwise—but I can tell that's changed since I looked upon her.

Now I get why my fugitive brother is so happy on his keffing farm out on a backwater planet in the middle of nowhere. He gets his mate all to himself, no questions asked. Seems like a pretty good deal right about now.

I watch my female to make sure she's comfortable, and then turn to look at my crew. I can feel their judgment even before I meet their eyes. They don't like this. I can't say I blame 'em. I'm not sure I like it, either—I just know I have no choice in the matter. She's mine.

Sentorr crosses his arms and just looks at me.

Alyvos scowls, his jaw clenched.

Tarekh just looks amused, as if I'm still playing a game or two of sticks and someone's suddenly gotten the upper hand on me. Feels a bit like that, too, I have to admit. I feel completely lost but in a good way.

"Well?" Sentorr asks. "Going to explain yourself?"

I glance over at the female, but she's still sleeping, her eyes closed. "He wasn't kind to her. I couldn't leave her there with him." Everything in me rebels against the very idea.

"Not our fight," Sentorr says.

"It is now. She belongs to me."

Tarekh's eyes widen. "It's like that, then? You're keeping a human pet, then?"

They misunderstand. I scrub a hand down my face, wondering how much I should admit to. "Not exactly. She's her own person, not a pet. She's just as intelligent as you or I, and I don't plan on owning her or forcing her to submit to me like Jth'Hnai wanted to do to her."

Tarekh laughs. "Then you mean..."

I shrug. I don't feel the need to answer him. Not exactly. Not when Alyvos is giving me such a horrified look. He'll just have to get used to the idea.

"You could have left her on the station," Sentorr protests.

"So someone else can grab her and force her into slavery?" I snort and shake my head. "You know as well as I do that she wouldn't last five minutes on her own. Not without a protector."

"It's a good thing you're so kind-hearted," Tarekh says slyly.

I shoot him a quelling look.

"The plan was just for the crystal," Alyvos bites out, spreading his hands in frustration. "Now we have most of the crystal, we've pissed off our contacts, and we've stolen a contraband pet—"

"Not a pet," I correct him again. I'm getting irritated at them. I knew they'd have a hard time with this, but for kef's sake, it's not like I'm making her captain and giving her a share.

Least, not yet.

"I can hear everything you're saying," the female murmurs in a low, sleepy voice. "I'm right here and I'm not an idiot. I have a translator in my ear and it's telling me everything while I'm trying to take a nap."

Tarekh laughs. Sentorr looks like he sucked on something sour. Alyvos scowls at me like it's my fault.

"Go back to sleep, little one," I tell her. "It's going to be a while before we get out of the surge."

"Is that like hyperspace?" She yawns and then blinks at me sleepily. A moment later, she curls her legs under her in the chair, all dainty elegance, and I cannot help but be utterly fascinated.

Little Kivian is as well.

"Hyperspace?" Sentorr echoes with disdain. "Never heard of such a thing." He looks at me. "And you think humans aren't primitive? Does she imagine us just flying through space on fossil fuels or some other crude nonsense?"

"Maybe she thinks we're gods," Alyvos continues, picking up the thread of conversation. "Maybe she's going to worship us."

Tarekh seems amused at the thought. "I don't know if I'm keen on being worshiped. Perhaps—"

"Dude, seriously." The female opens her eyes and gives us a dark glare. "Still right here. You're all still talking over me like I'm the family dog."

I chuckle, even though I don't know what a dude or a dog is. All I know is that her indignation is charming. "You'll have to forgive us if we're not being proper hosts, little one. It's been a long time since we carried a passenger."

"Longer since we did it without pay," Sentorr grumbles.

"You could ask me my name," she says calmly. "That'd be a start."

I'm utterly chagrined that we haven't asked about herself, but I try to cover it. "What, you mean FuckYou isn't your true name? I'm shocked."

Her lips twitch with amusement, her body pressed back against my captain's chair. The surge shakes and pushes at us as we shuttle through space at high speed. It's only years of living on ships that allow me to keep my balance as the deck makes minute shifts under my feet over and over again and my ears pop repeatedly. I can only imagine the force it's inflicting on her smaller frame. It's not safe to retreat to personal quarters yet, but I wish it was. She looks as if she could sleep, and I can't wait to be the one that gets to wake up next to her.

"Well?" I prompt when she doesn't seem to be in any hurry to answer. "What do we call you?"

She yawns again. "Fran. My name is Fran."

Fran. Fran. A strange, discordant sounding name for such a

lovely, delicate being. I commit it to memory, even though she will always be "little one" to me. "Very well," I murmur. "Fran it is."

FRAN

I'm so tired. For the first time in what feels like forever, I can sleep and not worry about being groped or molested. There's a weird, almost centrifugal force pushing down on me as we fly through space. "Surging," they call it. Whatever it is, it's exhausting. It constantly presses on me and makes my muscles feel as if they're straining even when I'm sitting still. Despite that, I can't help but fall asleep. I feel strangely safe despite being in the presence of four big blue aliens.

And I'm trying not to overthink what the big one said about me. Kivian. That's his name. The one that gave me the shirt and lets me sit in his chair while he looms nearby, half naked and domineering without being pushy. It's a strange combination, but then again, a lot about today has been strange. I drift in and out of sleep, but his words keep echoing in my mind.

You know as well as I do she wouldn't last five minutes on her own.

I don't plan on owning her or forcing her to submit to me.

She belongs to me.

She belongs to me.

She belongs to me.

The words ring in my head but without the menacing underlying meaning that Froggy's words had when he said the same thing. Kivian's words were said in an affectionate tone, and he's not treating me the same as the other. Still, I can't let my guard down entirely, but I'm also low on options. He's not wrong that I wouldn't last five minutes on my own. I'd be stranded in outer space with no money, no clothes, and only the barest hope of communication. Plus, if everyone looks at me as little more than an exotic puppy, I'm not going to get far.

I might not like or trust these men, but for the moment, I'm stuck with them.

I dream about food, and being held down. The dreams aren't good ones, and I wake up constantly, jerked alert by the panic of being captured again, only to find that I'm still in Kivian's chair, the endless push of the "surge" ongoing. It doesn't make for restfulness, and the only reason I'm able to relax is that Kivian's butt is directly in front of me as he sits on the dashboard in front of his chair, his tail flicking back and forth as he and his crew chat in low voices.

I wake up a short time later, gasping, my ears feeling unclogged for the first time in what must be hours. I rub one lobe, curious, and then I realize we've stopped. A jaw-breaking yawn escapes me and I sit upright. "Are we there?"

"Define 'there,' little one?" Kivian moves to the side of my chair, amusement on his blue face. He's fascinating to look at, I have to admit. I've never seen an alien before, but if I had to create one to make him "just different enough" to be alien and just sexy enough to be attractive, it'd probably look like him. His features are bigger than a human's, his cheekbones and chin more pronounced. His forehead is ridged and plated like his chest, but his eyes are dark and liquid and warm. And his lips...sheesh.

Those lips are just unfair. I don't even know why I'm thinking about them.

But his response makes me worry just a little about the state of things. Where *is* "there," exactly? I'm now on an alien spaceship with these guys, and I'm just as clueless as to my fate as before. I sit upright, uneasy. "Where are we going?"

"You mean in the next few minutes or in general?"

I purse my lips and give him a stern look. He seems to love to tease, this Kivian. Too bad for him I'm not in the mood. Being kidnapped by aliens, sold to a frog-man and then snatched a second time has worn me out. "Yes to both?"

He inclines his head, as if acknowledging his answer was a crappy one. "Overall, we are heading to the nearest asteroid belt. We're going to get there, cloak our ship so it reads as just another object in a sea of floating objects, and then we're going to lie low until the ooli are off our trail. That might be weeks. It might be a month. It might be two days...but I doubt it'll be two days. Not with the amount of crystal we got away with." He gives me a devilish grin. "That one's going to sting for a while."

"And after that, you still won't take me to Earth?"

Kivian crosses his arms over his chest and shakes his head. "I'm afraid not, little one. It's a dangerous trip from here, and while I like you very much, I don't think my crew is ready to risk their lives for you. For now, you're with me."

Well, at least he's honest. It isn't the first time he's given me the un-sugar-coated version of events, and it makes me trust him a little more. I'd rather know what I'm up against than be lied to. I rub my tired, aching head and then realize that the awful pressure has eased. I look around in surprise. "Have we stopped thrusting?"

"Surging?" he corrects, amused.

I can feel my cheeks getting hot. God, did I just say *thrusting*? Kill me now. "That was what I meant."

"Of course," he says smoothly. "And yes, we've stopped for now. We're at a cruising speed that will still enable us to outrace anyone that tries to follow. It'll take a while yet for us to reach our destination."

"Our destination being the asteroid belt. Right." I stifle an exhausted yawn, and to my chagrin, my stomach growls loudly. "Sorry about that."

"I should be the one apologizing. You must be hungry. Come." He extends one big hand to me, and I study him. So different and yet so similar to humans. If it weren't for the three fingers and the blue tint of his skin, I'd think it was a human hand.

I unbuckle my seatbelt and put my hand into his...and I'm surprised at the soft, velvety texture of his skin. It's like suede. No...the soft cloth they use to buff cars. Chamois. That's it. Touching him is amazing and I have to resist the urge to pet him like an idiot.

"Everything all right?" He notices my hesitation.

I want to snatch my hand from his grip in embarrassment. "Yes. Sorry. I'm just tired."

"And hungry," he agrees, holding me up firmly when I get to my feet and then wobble. It seems that "surging" takes a lot out of a person, even when you're just sitting down through the whole thing. I feel like I ran a marathon in the dead of summer. I'm exhausted.

When he puts a steadying arm around my waist, I lean against him. It's not like I have a choice. My legs feel too noodly and weak to support me.

"Come," he says gently. "We'll get some food into you and then we're off."

Off? I remember that I asked him where we were going in both the next few minutes and in general, and he only answered the "in general" part. "Off to where?"

Kivian grins down at me, displaying sharp fangs. "Why, to my bed of course."

All of a sudden, the supportive hand on my waist feels less than comforting. I jerk away—and nearly stumble backwards. "You said I wasn't your slave!"

"You're not." His voice is calm, the smile on his face engaging despite his words.

"Then what makes you think I'm going to sleep with you?"

"It beats the floor, for one. And this is a cruiser-style ship." He spreads his hand, gesturing at the narrow hallway we've entered. "Set up for four basic crew—captain, nav, medic, and mech. There's really nowhere else for you to sleep." He puts a hand to his mouth conspiratorially. "And I don't think the others would prefer to share."

I'm confused. I frown at him, trying to piece together what he's saying in my tired mind.

He sees my hesitation and says gently, "No sex. But I'm serious when I say there are not enough beds. The floors are cold and hard, and I promise I won't touch you without your consent."

"And I'm supposed to trust that?" I retort, helpless.

"You do not have to trust it," he agrees, putting a firm hand around my waist again. "But look at it this way. If I wanted to mate with you, I've had many chances already." He begins to move down the hall again, half-dragging, half-guiding me along with him. "Why would I need to take you with us—and infuriate my crew—just to get into your cunt when I could have done so in front of Jth'Hnai?"

I can't pronounce that frog's name, no matter how many times I hear it. But...he's got a point. "You said you didn't like an audience," I grumble. I still don't trust this, but I might not have a choice in the matter.

"I really don't," he agrees cheerfully. "I am many things, but an exhibitionist is not one of them." He gestures at a recess down the hall that I'm starting to recognize as a ship door. "This is where our mess is. Come. You can eat and I can tell you all about how I won't touch you without your permission."

"You keep adding that 'your permission' thing," I point out.

He glances down at me, and his eyes are warm, his smile inviting. "That is because, my sweet Fran, I plan on having your permission. Just not today."

6

KIVIAN

$\mathcal{T}$he little human female is clearly flustered by my words. The color gets high in her cheeks and her eyes flash at me even as her body stiffens. She's fascinating to watch, because her round, smooth face is so mobile. Her expressions are pure joy to observe, and I want to see all of them cross her face.

Well, no. I don't want to see her upset or scared. But full of joy and laughter? Yes. Full of desire? Yes. Full of anticipation as I push my cock into her warm, inviting cunt?

Oh yes.

I force myself to pay attention despite those distracting thoughts and gesture over the panel to open the mess hall of the *Fool*. Inside, it's as neat and tidy as Sentorr's cabin, which tells me he must be on cleaning duty this week. If it was Tarekh's week, the place would look like the disaster the big male leaves behind in any room he enters. I move my female toward one of the stools at the table, and then have to lift her into the seat when it becomes obvious that she won't be able to get atop it on her own—her human legs are too short.

"Wait here," I tell her. "I'll fix you something to eat. Do your people have any allergies?"

"If I say peanuts, does that mean anything to you?" Fran asks in a wry voice.

I hesitate. She has a point. I don't want to poison her with mesakkah food, but I also know she needs to eat. "What did the others feed you back at the station? The ooli?"

She shrugs. "The froggy guy just bought me a few hours before we got there. He didn't feed me anything. Before that, I was in a big pen of some kind in another station. They gave me these bar things." She gestures with her hands to indicate the size, then wrinkles her nose. "They were terrible. Please tell me all your food isn't like that."

It sounds like they were giving her livestock rations. Anger burns in my belly. To think that my mate, my sweet, fragile female, was treated like a mindless animal. "No, our food isn't like that," I say, my tone curt. "I'll fix you what we eat, and just let me know if you have any reactions to it. If there's itching or burning in your throat or you find it difficult to breathe, we'll wake up Tarekh and make him do a full allergen panel on you." I open one of the cabinets and survey our rations. As we tend to spend most of our time in space and our ex-military mech is also the one in charge of supplies, it tends to be rather dull, food-wise. I rummage around the neatly stacked nutrient choices, trying to find one that'll be appealing to an alien palate. "Do you prefer sweet or savory?"

"I prefer anything," Fran says. "I'm starving."

I pick a savory meat broth with chski pickles, a specialty of my home planet and a personal favorite of mine. It's from Alyvos's personal stockpile, but I'll pay him back. As I wait for the dispenser to heat the product, I contemplate sharing my quarters with Fran.

It doesn't matter that we won't mate. Not yet. She's mine and I can be patient. When she loses her fear, that's when I can woo her. Until then, my task is to make her as comfortable as possible. My quarters are the nicest, and my bed is big enough to sleep two. That's not the reason I want her with me, of course. I don't point out that we could clear out some space in the cargo bay and make her a pallet. She's my mate and she deserves better…and I want her next to me. I want to wake up to the sight of her. I want to breathe in her scent, have her soft hair spread across my sheets. I want her limbs tangled in the bedcovers next to mine.

I want her to roll over and press her breasts to my chest and demand that I mate with her.

One thing at a time, of course, I tell myself. There's plenty to keep us busy for the next while. Sentorr and Alyvos will be switching off on shifts to keep us stealthed, changing our ship's signal on a regular basis so we don't leave an obvious trail. Tarekh's been complaining about repairs that need to be done to the *Fool* once we're between jobs, and I've got a few palms to grease and people to reassure. There's the station security at Haal Ui, for starters, who need to be bribed to look the other way when it comes to our records. There's the kaskri, who need to be reassured that their shipment is on the way, even though we're taking the slow route. Then there's fake documents that need to be cross-checked against databases and uploaded to mask our identities in the next system and a host of other small tasks before we can move on from hiding.

Sometimes it's exhausting being a pirate. I don't mind it, though, because I've never been one to play too close to the rules. I prefer making my own rules, and I like doing my own thing. We don't hurt anyone, at least not physically. Their pockets (and their pride) are entirely different matters. The ooli are bound to be furious once they're found, and I have no doubt there will be a huge bounty on my head. There won't be for Fran, since she's contraband, but they'll be asking about her in the right circles.

I need to make sure she stays safe, and as long as she's with me, she's safe.

Of course, as long as she's with me, that doesn't mean I can't woo her, charm her and make her comfortable. I want her to let her guard down so when I flirt with her, she welcomes my hints. I want to see her smile at me with sleepy eyes as she strips off her clothing and bares her soft, delicate body to my gaze...

I glance over at Fran, who's gone quiet. She's sitting at the table, her feet swinging like a child's on the too-tall chair. Her face looks hollow with exhaustion, and as I watch, she rubs her ear, where the translation bulb juts from her head.

I'm a keffing asshole.

Here I am, thinking of taking her to bed and plotting out how I'm going to spend my time seducing her when she's miserable and has that thing sticking out of her head. It can't be comfortable. They're not meant for the wearer's ease, after all. I grab the bowl of soup and set it down in front of her, then place a hand on her shoulder. "Eat. I'll be right back."

"Where are you going?" She ignores her bowl and looks at me with alarm. It's clear she doesn't want to be abandoned again, not after she's determined that I'm safe. I decide I like that.

"I'll be right back," I promise her. "I'm not abandoning you."

She looks for a moment as if she'll protest, but then she nods and picks up the bowl, hunger winning over concern. Fran takes a sip of it, and I watch her cautiously to see if she has any reaction to it. When she makes a sound of pleasure and drinks more, I find myself both pleased and fascinated by the way her throat works. My cock throbs with the little noises she makes and I want to push another bowl into her hands and feed her more...and I want to drag her to my bed and strip my shirt off of her body.

All in time, I remind myself. There's no pleasure in it if she's not willing and just as eager as me. And for now, my female is tired and hungry and needs rest...and she needs that awful thing removed from her ear. I head to Tarekh's medbay, and when the doors open, I sigh at the mess in there. It's going to take me a keffing hour to find anything, much less the equipment I need.

It actually only takes about fifteen minutes to locate a medtool that can be used to extract the translator, but when I return to the mess hall, her head is down on the table, her bowl empty. Her eyes are closed and she's asleep, the translator poking out. I move next to her and touch a hand to her back. "Fran."

She jerks awake, terror in her eyes as she sits bolt upright. It takes a moment for her to focus in on me, and then she calms, taking a deep breath. "Sorry. I must have fallen asleep."

My chest aches at that fleeting moment of fear on her face. Protectiveness surges through me and I vow no one will ever touch this human—my human—again. They're going to have to get through me first. "That took a little longer than expected. My apologies." I hold up the medtool. "I'm going to need you to hold still for this."

Fran eyes me warily. "What is *that* for?"

"To get that thing out of your ear. It's not..." I struggle to find the right word for it.

"Humane?" she offers.

We don't have a word like that in our language, but once she says it, it makes sense. "Yes. Humane. The rest of us can pull your language from a download, and we'll get you a chip—a very painless chip, I might add—when we go into port next." I move forward and put my fingers under her chin. "Now, hold still."

She closes her eyes, dark lashes fanning down, and I'm momentarily fascinated by how lovely and delicate she is. Ah, my heart. To think that such a short time ago, it was all mine. Now it belongs to her as surely as if she reached into my chest and grabbed it with her small fingers. Didn't take long, either. My brother and I always teased my father about how fast and hard he says he fell for my mother.

I understand completely now.

Fran holds completely still, clutching at one of my wrists as I use the medtool. Brave, and yet she trusts me. I'm filled with pride. "All done, I think." I give the translator bulb a gentle tug, and it falls free from the dainty shell of her ear, leaving behind only a few scars and some redness. "Better now?"

She pulls away, touching her ear, and a little smile curves her mouth. "Much better. I hated that thing." A flash of unease crosses her face. "You won't talk around me though, will you? Like I'm not here? Just because I'm not wearing it?"

"You have my word," I vow to her. I'll let the rest of the crew know in the morning.

"Thank you. It's kind of hurtful when people talk over you like you're nothing more than a pet."

I'm ashamed to be included in that category. I'll just have to make it up to her. "Never again," I promise. "Do you want more food, or do you want to sleep?" *Or do you want me to hold you close and stroke your body until you sigh with pleasure?* I keep that last part to myself, because I know the answer it'll get.

"Sleep, I think." Her eyelids are drooping.

"Of course." I help her down off the stool and then keep a hand on her shoulder as I escort her down the narrow halls of the *Fool* to my quarters. The captain's apartments are in the belly of the ship. The low hum of the engines is most obvious here, but I like the sound of them. They lull me to sleep and I'm instantly awake the moment something sounds off. My cabin's the largest one on the ship, and because I'm a spoiled sort of male, I've spared no expense. I open the door and hope she's impressed with my furnishings. I'm not one for spareness, unlike Sentorr. I like the heaps of plush, down-filled cushions on my bed, the carved wood chair in the corner that's a priceless antique from Mii, and the fact that I have silken wall hangings from Homeworld, and a delicately crafted sticks table in the corner that comes straight from Ooli itself. My dressing closet hangs open, and it's stuffed to the brim with expensive clothing and boots, because I do like my luxuries.

She merely yawns and moves forward, tugging at something around her neck. "That the bed?"

"It is." I watch, amused, as she wanders toward it and drops something on the floor—the necklace that Jth'Hnai gave her, the one with his house symbols on it. I casually bend over and scoop it up as she climbs into bed, shoving aside my expensive pillows and clearing out a spot on the bed for herself. This necklace is going straight into the recycler. Jth'Hnai's never going to see her again. She's all mine now.

Fran takes one priceless, hand-embroidered by monks pillow and thumps it hard, then rests her head on it. "Do you have extra blankets?"

"I have the finest weave from Albaat," I tell her, picking up a throw I stole from a raid not too long ago.

She wrinkles her nose at it. "Looks scratchy."

"It's not supposed to be used, but admired."

Fran snorts and tucks her legs under the hem of my oversized shirt, her body curled into a ball. "Can I have one that's less fine of a weave and more of a blanket I can use?"

I chuckle and reach over her on the bed. "You can use mine."

"We're not sharing," she warns me immediately.

"I know." I gesture at the Albaat blanket in my hands. "I get the scratchy one."

A smile touches her mouth, and then she closes her eyes, snuggling into the pillow, wrapped in my bedding. It's the prettiest sight I've ever seen and I'm transfixed. I can't help but stare. She's perfect. Seeing her safe and relaxed in my bed has me feeling the strangest sort of contentment ever...mixed in with the most raging cock-stand ever.

Looks like I'm sleeping in my clothes tonight.

I unbuckle my boots and replace them carefully in my closet, then throw a shirt on over my chest, because I must be insane. But I don't want her to be frightened of me. I want Fran to know that she can trust me with her life, and if that means sleeping in layers for the next while, that's what it means.

But I'm not going to give way to her entirely, of course. She's going to sleep next to me. A male's got his limits, after all. I climb into the bed and lie back, closing my eyes and waiting. I can feel her stiffen in the bed next to me. That's to be expected. Eventually she'll realize I don't mean her harm and she'll relax.

Her tension continues for long moments, and I try to even out my breathing so she'll realize that all I want to do is sleep. After a minute, she turns over and I feel her shifting in the bed. A second later, a pillow jams up against my arm.

It takes everything I have not to burst out laughing. She's making a pillow barrier in the bed between us, like a child. Like that would solve anything if I had it in my mind to rape her. "You do realize that won't exactly protect you?" I murmur.

"Yeah, well, it makes me feel safe," she says, and jams another pillow between us.

"Do whatever you like, if it'll make you feel better."

The next pillow goes over my face, and then I can't help but burst out laughing.

My Fran is a fiery one. I like that.

7

FRAN

I've slept for the first time in what feels like weeks. I wake up with a yawn and roll over in bed. It's so damn comfortable that I don't want to get up. I'm surrounded by pillows, and the blankets I'm curled up in are the softest I've ever felt. I glance up at the ceiling sleepily, eyeing the stars and nebulae that look like they're spilling across the black sky. I know that's not a window but a screen, but it's still pretty. I could stay in bed like this all day, just curled up and...safe.

A low snore touches my ears.

Oh yeah.

With a little frown, I pull back one of the pillows in my "fortress." Kivian's on the other side, eyes closed, mouth slightly parted in his sleep. There's a hint of fang peeping out from under his upper lip, and his expression is completely relaxed. If he's faking it, he's doing an amazing job. I watch him for a long moment, and when he starts to gently snore again, I realize he's definitely asleep.

This gives me a chance to study him without being obvious.

It's so interesting, because unlike the frog-guys, Kivian could pass for human...ish. His features are very similar to mine. He's got near-human bone structure, just supersized. His forehead is strangely plated and striated, and his horns jut from his hairline. They're enormous, curling beasts of horns, and I'm not entirely sure how he manages to sleep. Of course, I notice the pillows seem to be small and he has one strategically placed under his neck to prop it up. Interesting. His lashes flutter with a dream, and his mouth moves ever so slightly.

And then he snores again.

I can't help but silently chuckle at that. He looks so human in this moment. Blue, yes. Seven foot tall, yes. Horns and tail? Yes. But he sleeps like anyone else, and it's comforting to see.

He also seems like he's going to be sleeping for a while, and I have to pee. I silently get up, wrap my blanket tight around my body, and explore his cabin, trying to remember how to operate the "water closet" as he called it. It takes me a little fiddling and button-pushing until I figure it out, and then I give myself a quick splashed bath in one of the sinks in the bathroom, hoping I'm not using the alien version of a bidet. I head toward his closet, because I'm tired of being naked-ish. He can donate another shirt to the cause.

A few moments later, I wonder if I'm looking in the wrong place. There's a lot of clothing hung up in the nook that I could have sworn was his closet, but I can't make heads or tails of any of it. Nothing looks like a regular shirt or pants. There are huge swaths of fabric, tiny ties, and fastenings. So many fastenings. I don't even know what I'm looking at, and I touch one sleeve—at least I think it's a sleeve—with a frown. It looks nothing like the shirt I'm wearing. Of course, now that I examine the intricate folds of the shirt I'm wearing, it does look like it has a lot of ties. Do I take it apart to try and figure out if it matches the others?

But then what if I'm left with nothing but a big decorative hanky to wear?

Then...it would be the same as what I wore yesterday when he rescued me? Which was close to nothing? *Duh, Fran.*

"You're staring very, very hard at my shirts," a sleepy voice murmurs. "Don't tell me. You disapprove of my fashion choices."

I glance over at the bed. Kivian's sat up in the blankets, a floppy lock of dark hair falling over his brow. He scratches at the shaved sides of his head, looking for all the world like a non-morning-sort of person, and then rubs his chest. It's plated like his forehead, and I can see plates along his biceps as well. Fascinating. Of course, now I'm staring. I force myself to make eye contact with him so he knows I wasn't creeping on him. "I'm trying to figure out if you have anything I can borrow."

"You can borrow any of it, of course," he says with a yawn. "You're my guest. You're entitled to whatever you like."

"Except a trip back to Earth," I jab, but then regret it the moment I say it. He's been upfront with me about things. I can't hate on him for not wanting to risk his life.

"Except that," he agrees, sleepy and good-natured. "But my clothes? You can have all of them and I shall go around naked."

"No thanks," I tell him, keeping my tone light. "I vote that we both remain completely clothed."

"If we must." He yawns again and climbs out of the bed. I skitter toward the closet, alarmed, but I'm relieved to see that he's still wearing pants, if not the shirt he went to bed in last night. He pads past me with heavy feet, smacking his lips, and heads for the water closet. I watch his tail swish as he disappears inside and he acts completely uninterested in me and more interested in his morning rituals.

Not that that's a bad thing. It's just...strange. For the last week I've been the object of an untold number of rapey leers, gropes, catcalls, and lewd gestures. I almost feel out of balance when someone treats me normal. Like I'm a roommate.

It feels like a trick.

I wait, watchful, until he emerges from the water closet. His eyes look a little brighter and his hair's been combed into place. He heads towards me and I clutch the neck of my borrowed shirt-dress and jolt away from him...only to watch as he picks out a piece of fabric and pulls it from its place amongst all the other clothing. "I told you I wouldn't hurt you," Kivian says calmly.

"You also said I belonged to you. You told everyone that," I remind him.

"I did. We're a covetous lot, we mesakkah." He shrugs. "I didn't mean it. I just wanted to get you away from Jth'Hnai."

"You told your men I was yours, too, you liar."

"Did I?" He grins over at me and runs a big blue hand down the fabric in his hand. "Perhaps I did. But let me reassure you that I don't intend on harming you. You're safe with me."

I cross my arms over my chest, skeptical. "How do I know you're not lying?"

"Because I already would have had you under me, screaming with pleasure, if I'd intended on taking you forcefully." He gives me a sultry look under lidded eyes. "You think there aren't females out there that are telling me no with their mouth and yes with their eager hands?"

"Ew? I'm telling you no with everything."

Kivian grins, all boyish charm once more. "Which is why I'm not touching you. You and I, we're just friends. Nothing more. You have my word on it. Now, shall I show you how to wear one of these shirts properly? They're very popular in six different systems, but you truly do need a tutorial in how to lace one up."

I can continue to spit anger at him, or I can take him up on his friendly offer. I hesitate, still clutching my shirt. Truth is, I don't know if I can trust him. Or trust anyone. But...he's not wrong in that he could have hurt me already and didn't. The pillow fortress remained intact all night. Even when we were in Froggy's room and he could have raped me without a second thought, all he did was flirt...and stall.

"Please don't betray my trust," I whisper as I move forward, choosing to take him at his word. "I need someone I can count on."

"My dear, sweet Fran," he murmurs, and the look he gives me is intense. "I would sooner die than betray you. Know that for a fact."

And somehow, I believe him.

KIVIAN

I suppose it's time I introduce Fran to the crew.

They already know who she is, of course. And she's aware of them. But I feel a more formal introduction will let all parties get used to the thought of being around each other, since we'll probably be in the asteroid belt for an unspecified amount of time.

It's odd, though. I feel startlingly possessive. I don't *want* to introduce her to the crew. I want to keep her all to myself, in my bed, wearing my clothing. I knew I'd feel a little possessive about her. I'm a mesakkah, after all. But right now I just want to growl and wrap my tail around her and glare at anyone that even thinks of coming to my door and bothering us.

But it's a small ship. I guess I can't do that.

Fran gives me a curious look as I finish knotting the last few cords of her sleeve. "You seem like you're in a bad mood."

"I'm not, my sweet," I reassure her. "I'm merely thinking."

"Don't strain yourself."

I chuckle. "It's time you meet my crew, since we'll all be living together for a while."

She frowns in my direction. "I met them, didn't I? Three big blue guys. Unless there's more somewhere?"

"That's it. We run a small crew. But you should learn names. It'll give them a chance to get to know you and it'll make everyone more comfortable." Plus, it'll set the tone for the rest of this trip. I don't want someone treating her like a pet when it's clear she's as smart as everyone else.

"Can't I just stay in here with you?"

I bite back my groan of need. I wish. "This won't take long. I promise. Then you're free to roam about."

She studies me a moment longer, and then shrugs. "Lead the way, then."

I put a hand to her back and immediately feel a surge of need. Gods, if touching her like this is making me hard, it's going to be agony keeping myself under control.

She steps forward and her rounded bottom brushes against the front of my trou. Ah, kef. Everything in my body lights up, and my cock grows achingly hard. Fran skitters away from me, her eyes wide. It's clear she felt that.

Of course she felt it. My cock feels as if it's ten lengths long, all thanks to her presence. I decide to play the idiot. "Problem?"

Fran blinks at me. I can see the wheels turning in her mind, but after a moment, she narrows her eyes at me and shakes her head. "No, I'm good."

I gesture at the door, feeling like a fraud. "Shall we?"

She nods and moves ahead, and I notice she's deliberately keeping more space between us this time so a repeat doesn't happen. My smart, cautious Fran.

For the next while, I take her around the ship, showing her what's behind each door, the things she shouldn't touch for her own safety, and introducing each member of the crew as we come across them. Sentorr's on the bridge and keeps his replies to Fran very curt. It's clear he disapproves of her presence and she senses it, though she's polite to him. Tarekh is, well, he's Tarekh. He's laughing and easygoing and despite that, I can tell Fran is intimidated by him. He's a big male, with a face only a blind mother could love. She'll get used to him. It'll just take a bit more time.

Alyvos is the only one left, and I expect them to get along about as well as anyone else does with Alyvos—with gritted teeth and sheer tolerance. The navigator's in the cargo bay, taking stock of our crystals. He glances up at me when we enter, then nods. He gives Fran a quick nod too, then goes back to work. Alyvos is dependable because it's never about emotion, just about work. "Captain. Human."

"She has a name," I tell him.

"I know she does. I just don't know it." He doesn't even look up from his data pad.

To my surprise, Fran gives a musical little laugh. "I don't mind 'human.' It beats 'pet' any day."

"Mm." I'm strangely jealous that he got her to laugh when everything I do terrifies her. "How are things looking, Alyvos?"

"Shipment's shy a few thousand crystals, if I don't miss my guess. I'm counting everything to log it, but I won't know for sure until I'm done." He gives me a quick look. "If you're looking for numbers, it's going to be a few."

"Take your time."

Fran steps forward. "Can I help?"

My jealousy surges through me when Alyvos looks up with a pleased expression. "No," I say quickly, stepping between them. "She's mine."

"What?" Fran asks.

"Mine to show around," I amend smoothly. And then I glare at my navigator, as if daring him to contradict me.

He just smirks.

I know I'm acting like a possessive fool. I don't care. I want to be the only one Fran smiles at. The only one that touches her. If I could chase everyone else away from her right now, I would. It's not reasonable, of course.

No one ever said I was a reasonable male. All I know is that she's mine and no one's getting near her.

8

KIVIAN

*I*t takes about two days for the hunted look to leave Fran's lovely face. It takes about two days and one hour for Fran to charm my crew. I know they're going to get along just fine when I go into the mess one morning to find her arguing with Sentorr over the best-tasting meal packs and Tarekh's laughing at both of them because Fran's been eating my supplies instead of theirs. It seems that she likes the same salty noodles I do.

"She's got good taste," I tell them with pride, even if it does leave me with nothing but the leftovers. I don't mind. Not for Fran.

It's been days and she's already wormed her way into my heart and soul. Hard to believe that I would fall so fast—no, "fall" isn't the right word. More like "crash." There was no in-between in Fran storming into my life and my falling in love with her. She's just suddenly everything. I think of her when I drift off to sleep, and she's the first thing on my mind when I wake.

Clearly she doesn't feel the same way about me yet, but she'll get there. How can she not fall for me? I'm incredibly charming. She's just stubborn, my Fran. She'll come around.

"I don't see how a pirate can spend so much damn time farting around with sleeves," she says, her hands on her hips as she glares into my closet. It's become one of her favorite pastimes—criticizing my wardrobe. "Don't you have pirate-y things to do other than spend hours lacing up your sleeves?"

"Like what?" I lounge on one of my chairs since I've learned that lounging in bed makes her skittish.

"I don't know. Whatever space pirates do?" She casts me a look over her shoulder. "Make someone walk a space plank? Board a ship? Something?"

"First of all, a space plank is just ridiculous," I tell her as she picks the least complicated of my shirts and pulls it from the closet. "Second of all, why would we board someone else's ship? We're in hiding. You were never very good at hide-and-find as a child, were you?"

"Humans call it hide-and-seek, and I was very good at it," Fran tells me, and takes the shirt into the water closet with her to change. I wait until she returns a moment later, swimming in the fabric, and she comes to my side. "Show me the sleeves again?"

"It's a raithu knot," I tell her. "All the rage on Homeworld." I take several of the cords hanging from the sleeve fabric, and when she holds her arm out, I begin to tie them in place, creating the sleeve out of the puffs of fabric.

"Can I cut the shirt down into a dress for me?"

"Cut it?" I pretend horror at the thought. "Do you know how much this cost?"

"No?" She looks crestfallen. "Was it very expensive?"

"A year's wages for most workers, I imagine. I don't run amongst the lower-class circles, so I'm not entirely sure if that's accurate, but it's expensive, yes."

Poor Fran looks aghast at the thought. "All right, show me the knots again."

I do, and by the time the sleeves are done, she's twitching with impatience. It's adorable. I could watch her all day. In fact, I might just do that since there's nothing else to do...but wait. Once the sleeves are finished, she takes a braided cord and loops it tight around her waist, making a belt. My shirts are big enough that they fit her like dresses, and it's both erotic and adorable to see her clothed in nothing but my gear. Sentorr offered up a few old shirts, but I growled at him until he promised he wouldn't bring it up with her.

I like her wearing my things. She can dice them into pieces for all I care as long as they make her happy.

"So what's the plan today?" she asks, combing her hair as she peers into a mirror and then peeks over at me.

I shrug lazily and spread a hand. "This?"

Fran puts the comb down and frowns at me. "You mean there's nothing for you to do either?"

There's plenty, but I don't feel like it, not when she's so delightfully entertaining. "Either? Are you bored?"

She tilts her head and gives me a patient look. "You have *no* idea."

"Well then, what would you like to do?"

The little human sits in a chair across from me. "I don't know. There's not much for a captive to do."

I can feel myself frowning at her. "You're not a captive. You're a guest."

"Then take me home to Earth."

"Nice try, but no."

Fran makes an exasperated sound and then leans back, her arms crossed. I notice that she crosses her legs, too, and I'm fascinated by that elegant movement. "Then what do you do if you're stuck in a quiet ship all day?"

I shrug. "I catch up on paperwork. It's dreadfully boring, I know, but even a pirate has communications he has to answer." I think of my brother, who's sent another message that I haven't yet had a chance to respond to. He sent more pictures of tiny Kivita, my ugly, fascinating little namesake, and urged me to come out and visit them. I'll reply to him soon...when I have an answer. Right now I'm more focused on the female in front of me. "Sometimes I read a book."

She makes a face at me. "All your books are in a language I don't understand."

I chuckle. "Listen to music, then? Or I practice my sticks."

"Sticks?" Her brows furrow. "That's the game you were playing with Froggy, right?"

I incline my head at her. "That's the one."

"Can you show me how to play it?" She turns her chair to face me and gestures at the table between us. "We could play right here."

"Do your people have games of chance?" I'm constantly surprised by the things she tells me. Humans aren't nearly as primitive as I've been led to believe.

"Oh yeah. I'm pretty good at cards."

"Cards?" I give her a strange look. "You play with cards? Little pieces of paper? Why would you do something so foolish?"

"Are you kidding me? You guys play with sticks! Freaking sticks! Now who's the foolish one?" She sounds so indignant.

I burst into laughter. "Fair enough."

Her indignant look turns to a smile, and then she chuckles. "I guess they all sound silly when you break them down. All right, so show me how this works."

I tap a panel on the table and my favorite sticks set rises out of its storage place. "Well, as I like to say, it's all in the wrist."

She arches an eyebrow at me. "I feel like I've heard this one before."

I grin. "Perhaps you have. Shall I show you my technique?"

I expect her to make a scathing comeback, but she only leans in and gives me a sultry smile. "Show me what you've got, hot shot."

Her words make me fumble for the sticks case, and the playing pieces scatter across the table.

Fran's little laugh of amusement is utterly delightful, and I fumble a second time.

I don't even mind.

PLAYING sticks for hours a day becomes part of our new routine. Sometimes we play after we wake up and before we head out to the mess for breakfast. Sometimes we play after dinner, when all the work for the day is done and I have some time to myself. Fran doesn't have much to do, so she busies herself with hand-sewing a dress or two from my least-favorite shirts and she practices her sticks techniques. She looks forward to our gaming sessions every day, and I do as well. There's nothing I'd rather do than spend an evening with Fran, laughing and talking.

She's quickly become my favorite person to talk to. Not just because her acerbic sense of humor matches mine, but she's able to see things from an entirely different perspective than I can. She's also quick to let me know when my ego is getting in the way, and when such feedback might have irritated me if it came from Alyvos or Sentorr, Fran just makes me laugh and realize I'm being an ass.

I like learning about her, too. There's so much about human society that sounds both fascinating and odd, and our conversations sometimes highlight just how different our cultures are.

"So your brother's wife is pregnant?" she asks me one night as we play sticks. "How's that possible?"

I chuckle and give her a playful look. "Well, Fran, when a male and female love each other very much..."

She rolls her eyes. "Very funny."

"—they get together and purchase the finest plas-womb that the medics have to offer."

Her eyes widen. "Wait, what?" She looks startled. "They purchased a test-tube baby?"

"Actually, no. I think they're doing it the old-fashioned way." I think of Chloe's bloated stomach and suppress a male shudder of unease. "She's growing it in her stomach. I imagine there was some medical assistance, of course, but if you have enough credits, anything's possible."

Fran stares at me, her jaw hanging open.

"What?" I cast my sticks down and wait for her to take her turn.

"You're grossed out by it, aren't you? By her having a baby."

I frown and gesture at the gameboard in front of us. "Your turn. And no, I'm not 'grossed out.' It's just...unusual."

"Because of hygiene laws?"

"Among other things, yes. Most mesakkah females don't bother having their children naturally. Not when there's a perfectly good artificial womb waiting to be rented. You donate your biological information, pay a fee, and then you can pick up your child when it's ready."

"That's...weird."

"It's all very sanitary, I assure you."

She puts a hand to her stomach, disturbed. "I don't think I'd want to do that if I ever had a baby. I'd want to carry it if I could. Your homeworld's laws just seem so...cold."

A few weeks ago, I might have agreed with her. But since then, I've seen Fran's smiles and breathed in her scent. I've touched her soft skin and licked her thigh. To say that I'm hungry for more would be like saying the universe is vast. There's no end to how much I want her and crave her.

"They do seem like cold laws," I murmur. I think of Jutari and how happy he seems, how content. It's clear he doesn't think about sanitary laws. I do wonder how much happier we'd be as a people if we weren't so focused on disease. Interesting to think about.

Fran gives a little shake of her head and then casts down her sticks on the board. Her throw is terrible, but I can flub my next one so that she pulls ahead and the game continues a bit longer. It's cheating in a way, of course, but I look at it as practice. Who knows when I'll have to hoodwink the next target in a game? It's best to know how to play against anyone, even a terrible player.

Besides, nothing makes Fran laugh with more delight than when she "wins" against me. I'm addicted to that triumphant giggle.

"I can't imagine a society where you can't even kiss the person you love," she tells me, studying the table in front of us.

"Kiss?"

"A meeting of mouths. It's a show of affection amongst humans."

"Care to demonstrate?" I give her my best lazy grin, though my heart is pounding at the thought of her putting her plump lips against mine. Sanitary laws be keffed, I want to taste her.

But all she says is, "I'd hate to break your hygiene laws."

"I'm a pirate, my sweet. Breaking laws is what I do. Don't let that dissuade you from your goal."

She just wags a finger at me as if I'm being naughty. "You may be a pirate, but I'm not. I'm just a pirate's captive."

"Ah, yes, because I won't let you go back to Earth. Can't you just be a guest?" I pretend to study the table in front of us, though in truth I'm concentrating on Fran and her expression.

My human looks thoughtful. "But a guest is somewhere because they want to be there, right? So I can't say that I'm a guest, either."

"Then what are you?" I ask. *Other than mine, because I'm never letting you go.*

She purses her lips and thinks. "When I figure it out, I'll let you know."

9

FRAN

Sharing quarters with a big blue alien man proves to be a lot tighter than I originally anticipated. It's a small ship—and the captain's quarters aren't exactly enormous—so we're constantly running into each other or brushing up against each other.

One night, I'm getting ready for bed when I yawn and stretch. Kivian's nearby flipping through something on his data pad when he suddenly gets up from his desk and heads to the small water closet. As he walks, I can see the front of his trousers are tented with a rather obvious erection.

I swallow hard, wondering what I should say. Should I do anything? Ignore it? Pretend like I didn't see? Confront him? I think of the time that I brushed up against him and felt his erection rub against my backside. He'd acted like it was nothing and I thought I was mistaken.

There's no mistaking that bulge in the front of his pants.

Do I say something, though? We've got such a fragile balance. He's treated me like a welcome guest ever since I arrived, and even though my dreams—both day and otherwise—have been a little steamy, he's been the perfect gentleman.

And yet...

I nibble on a fingernail, thinking. Curiosity gets the best of me, and I creep toward the water closet on silent feet, and then lean closer, listening like the freak I am. It's quiet in there. Of course it is. It's probably soundproofed. Duh, Fran.

But then I hear it. The unmistakable slap of skin. A soft groan. Something shifts inside, as if a large body is leaning up against a counter.

My entire body flushes with awareness. Is he...touching himself in there? To me? Because I stretched?

I'm breathing hard at the thought, imagining it. My hand slides to the front of the long shirt I'm wearing as a dress. I could touch myself right now, masturbate like he is...

What's wrong with me? He's not shown any interest in me at all other than as a friend. What if this is a normal sort of thing for blue people? What if this is just another bodily function and I'm creeping on him like a pervert, imagining that big blue body covering mine? Imagining him leaning over me and nipping at one breast with those perfect lips of his...

I shouldn't be thinking about sex. Not after what I've been through. Maybe I'm messed up in the head after my ordeal. The thought's a sobering one, and I retreat back to the bed and pull the covers over me, tucking them under my chin and closing my eyes.

If he wanted to touch me, he would have...wouldn't he?

10

FRAN

Days Later

Kivian's started sleeping naked.

He asked me if he could, of course. He's a restless sleeper, and when I prodded him about it, he admitted that he's used to sleeping without clothing and that the fabric against his skin chafes and distracts him. So I told him he could sleep naked. I gave him permission.

We've been so friendly and so easy I didn't think it would mess with my mind.

Duh, Fran. Duhhhhhh.

I'm dying to look over. Nudge a pillow to the side. Get a little glimpse. Dying. *Dying.* But I can't bring myself to do it.

It feels like a betrayal of our friendship.

Dying, though. Like, is he as big—equipment-wise—as I think he is? He's seven feet tall, so he should be.

Duh, Fran.

Sometimes I tell myself one little peek won't hurt. But I can't bring myself to do it.

Just one little peek would answer so many questions.

But I can't. I just can't.

Gosh, I wish I could, though.

FRAN

J feel like I'm going to explode if something doesn't happen between us soon. Either I need to get over him, or I need to get whatever passes as an alien vibrator around here.

Something.

All I know is that I'm going crazy being around that big blue slab of delicious man and I don't know what to do. He's the one in control of my life, so I don't dare make a move. He hasn't indicated that he wants to touch me or be anything other than friendly.

I've never masturbated so hard—or so very furtively—in my life.

Something's got to change soon, I think, or I might snap and start dry-humping his leg like the oversexed poodle-fuck-toy I'm supposed to be.

FRAN

Three weeks later

I wake up with a yawn. It's early, the faux window in the room set to simulate a sunrise. Kivian's cabin doesn't actually have any windows at all, so the settings are based around what the user desires. I love waking up to a sunrise, and Kivian can sleep through pretty much anything, so the setting is set to my liking. I smile and watch the "sunrise" for a minute, admiring the thick, fluffy clouds. I don't even mind that the "sky" in the picture is a watery sort of green. It's the thought that counts.

Mornings are one of my favorite times on the *Fool*. None of these guys are early risers, so it's kind of "me" time. I like that little window of quiet. Normally I get up and start digging through the food stores and watch mesakkah vids, trying to pick up language basics. This morning, though, there's a big blue arm sprawled through the pillow fort, and I can't help but lift the pillow and peer over the side at Kivian.

No peeking any lower, of course. I still can't bring myself to do that even though I'm itching to check out his equipment. Doing so feels like it would break the fragile boundary we have on our relationship.

Kivian's a deep sleeper, all right. His mouth is parted, his hair disheveled over his hard, craggy brow. His clothes are pulled up, revealing washboard blue abs and obliques that make my fingers itch to touch them.

No lower, Fran, I tell myself. *That's a line you can't cross.*

Instead of scaring the shit out of me, it makes me feel...curious. Yeah, that's the word. Just curious. I squeeze my thighs together tightly.

Just curious. That's all.

I study him for a bit longer. It's been weeks since Kivian rescued me and brought me on the *Fool.* It's been three weeks for me to find my feet again. I've gone from having everything ripped out from under me to a weird semblance of normal, and I'm starting to like the new normal. It's different, but it's not all that bad. The crew's nice and I've fit in surprisingly well with them. I thought Kivian would be a problem with his early forwardness and chest-thumping declarations of MINE, but he's been a perfect gentleman so far. In all this time, he's cracked jokes, teased me, played games with me, been bossy and pushy, but he's never frightened me. He's never put a hand on me or even tried to get fresh with me. If anything, he dotes on me like a little sister.

I'm not sure how I feel about that.

I mean, I'm thankful. I'm *so* thankful he's not a big rapey son of a bitch. He's a big tease and a flirt, but he's not malicious and he's rarely serious. His personality is a fun one, and I actually enjoy being around him. I never thought I'd say that about an alien, but he's quickly becoming one of my best friends.

But as time passes, I'm not so sure if how I feel about him is "friendly" or something more. I find that I'm living for his laughs, his smiles. I eagerly anticipate each night in bed, hoping our limbs are going to brush against each other. I pace around the cabin all day because I feel it'd be too puppyish to follow him around the ship. I live for our sticks games. I'm addicted to his smell and switch out our pillows on the sly so I can breathe deep of his scent.

And I masturbate. Lord, how I masturbate. Daily. Sometimes twice a day. Once I even did it under the blankets while he slept. I can't help it.

I'm getting increasingly frustrated by the fact I've been firmly placed in "little sister" territory. Part of me thinks that I'm an idiot for even contemplating such a thing, but I can't help it. I'm fascinated by him and the fact that he made such strong claims about me belonging to him...and then doesn't act on it.

Not that I want him to act on it.

I think.

Actually I don't know what to think. All I know is that I'd love for him to grab me and pull me against him in a passionate kiss, and I'm pretty sure that's wrong of me to even contemplate.

I should be grateful that Kivian's treating me like an honored, welcome guest.

Yeah. Grateful. I'm feeling something, but I'm pretty sure it isn't gratitude. And I squeeze my knees tightly together again.

Kivian sleeps on, blissfully unaware of the conflict in my head as

I lie beside him. Ironic that I used to be annoyed that I had to share a bed with the guy. Now I get irritated that he's so good at staying on his side. Why can't he be a grabby snuggler?

I have issues.

Duh, Fran.

I crawl out of bed and pad toward the water closet in Kivian's apartments. I wash up and dress in one of the three outfits I can claim as my own. Since we haven't gone back to a station to restock, I have to make do with a few of Kivian's castoffs. His shirts have been converted to belted dresses, and I wear a pair of blowsy harem pants underneath. Apparently there's a type of material that will conform to the body of the wearer, but Kivian's a snob when it comes to clothing and all of his are tailored instead. So I get to dress like a hobo as I wander around the ship.

Truth is, I don't mind it. His clothes are comfy and soft, and they're made well even if they're a bit more intricate than I'm used to. The man likes his details, that's for sure. I do up the dozens of zig-zagging clasps up the front of my shirt dress and on the sleeves, then tie my hair back into a ponytail before heading to the front of the cabin. I glance back at him, wondering if I should just crawl back into bed and act on my impulses. Climb on top of him, confess my silly crush, and let the chips fall where they may.

But I don't. My safety here on the *Fool* depends on his goodwill, and I don't want to ruin that.

Kivian snores on, blissfully ignorant of my early-morning troubles. He doesn't even wake up when I signal over the doorlock that I want out and the portal opens.

I head to the mess for morning tea and breakfast. There's no coffee substitute, but there's a tea from an unpronounceable planet that tastes kind of like a paint-peeling version of Earl Grey, and it's quickly becoming my favorite. I make a cup of it and the strange soup they like for breakfast, and move toward the window so I can gaze out on my surroundings. It's an asteroid belt in the middle of the endless black of space, but I find it fascinating to watch anyhow. There's a distant nebula that looks like splashes of red and green stained the galaxy, and it's all a gorgeous sight. I might miss the sunrise or sunset back on Earth, but I'm getting pretty used to a view of the stars.

I could be happy out here if I can't make it back home again. I think.

It's taken me time to get used to the idea of not making it back to Earth. I sip my tea and contemplate the stars. Maybe it's that I was thrown into such a crazy situation that I never had time to properly grieve until I was already numb. Kivian and his crew have made it pretty clear that going back there isn't an option, no matter how much they like me. If they do, they run the risk of having the *Fool* confiscated and spending their days in an intergalactic prison. No one likes the idea of that. I can't let them destroy their lives just to...what? Bring me back to my dead-end receptionist job? My family is distant, my friends moved away after college, and my job sucks. I've had relationships, but nothing exciting. I've just been drifting since college, not really sure what to do with my life. Seems like fate stepped in and decided for me.

No matter how I look at it, Earth—and my life there—are distant memories.

But even if I want to stay, I'm not sure I can. Will they want to keep me? Right now I'm an interesting houseguest that tries to stay out of the way. I'm also going to eventually be a drain on resources, because I need to eat and breathe and use water.

There's no room for another bunk on the *Fool* and I don't know any useful skills.

I'm also a highly illegal species. All of this could be bad if they decide that I'm too much trouble, and no matter how much Kivian thinks of me as a little sister, even little sisters can get annoying.

My fate continues to hang by a thread. I'm still at the mercy of others.

That sucks.

Duh, Fran.

I finish my breakfast soup and put the cups in the cleanser. As I step out I head toward the bridge to see who's on shift. The cloaking signal that keeps the *Fool* hidden has to be continually re-jiggered, from how I understand it, so someone always remains on the bridge to keep an eye on things. It seems that even in their very high-tech society, some things just can't be trusted to a computer. I'm a little surprised to see the big medic, Tarekh, seated at Alyvos's seat at the bridge. "Is it your shift?" I ask him, moving to sit in Kivian's chair. Not because I envision myself as the captain, of course, but because I know he won't get mad if I curl up in it. I'm not there with the others yet.

Tarekh just shakes his head and leans back in Alyvos's spot, looking bored and lazy as lines of positions and codes and star charts scroll past his screen. "Just giving Alyvos a break today. He's a little frayed at the edges. Waiting's not his favorite thing to do."

I know how that goes. We've all been in limbo the past few weeks and it's making Alyvos and Sentorr prickly since they're the ones constantly monitoring the feeds. I think they've been expecting to get a go-ahead to move on from Kivian, but we're still waiting. I'm not exactly sure what we're waiting for, just that Kivian isn't ready to move us on yet. I worry that I'm the reason and the others are going to resent me. We all get along fine, but I know it can quickly flip if tempers get short. "Do you know what we're waiting for?"

Tarekh shrugs. "A sign that it's safe to move on and deliver our cargo. Don't worry. Kivian's got good instincts for this sort of thing."

I think about Kivian, asleep in the bed we share, and I get that weird flush moving through my body again. If he's got good instincts, then maybe I really am just a little sister to him or he'd have realized how much I'm hung up on him. Maybe he does realize it, and he's waiting for it to fade.

Ugh.

"You look unhappy," Tarekh points out as I chew on a fingernail. "Everything well?"

"Just thinking." When he gestures that I should continue, I hesitate and then decide to pour it out anyhow. I need to talk to someone. "Do your people have something we humans call Stockholm syndrome?"

"Never heard of it."

"It's where a woman falls in love with her captor just because he's the one with power over her. She glamorizes him and the control he has over her life, and she makes her entire world about pleasing him."

"Ah." He thinks for a minute and then studies me. "Yeah, we have a word for that."

"You do?"

"Foolish."

I frown at him and resist the urge to throw something at his big ugly head. "You suck."

"That's a human phrase saying I'm unpleasant, yes?" He chuckles.

"It's a real thing, you know."

"Oh, I know it's a real thing. We've a similar sort of mental illness in our civilization. In many civilizations, actually. It happens anytime there is power inequality. But I don't think that's what's happening to you."

I feel a little hint of relief, but I wonder if I'm being set up for another joke. "Why's that?"

He spreads a hand in a gesture toward me. "Think about your interactions with our dear captain. Let's say he comes in and tries to steal your morning meal as you eat it. What would you do?"

"Uh, slap his hand?" That's pretty much what I did yesterday when the exact same thing happened. Kivian just laughed at my outraged expression and tweaked my chin. For a man that goes on and on about hygiene laws, he sure does like touching me.

"Mmmhmm. And if he told you to cut your hair off because he likes a female with a shaved head?"

I chew on my lip. "I'd tell him to go kef himself—like you guys say —because I don't want a shaved head?"

He gives a sharp bark of amusement. "So you don't feel the need to change yourself to please him?"

I'm surprised he'd even ask such a thing. If there's a poster child for obedient slave, it's sure as shit not me. "God, no."

"Do you think you're in danger if you disobey him?"

I shake my head slowly. If anything, Kivian likes it when I'm sassy to him. My tart retorts sometimes get the biggest smiles...and I admit it makes me get a little mouthier as a result.

"Exactly. Then you don't have this 'syndrome' you think you do."

"Oh."

"You don't sound pleased."

I cross my arms under my breasts, thinking. "It was a lot easier when I thought it wasn't my own decision. I still feel it's wrong to have a crush on him."

"Why? Because he's blue?"

"No, because..." I stumble around for an answer and can't find one. Not really. Because he looks different? I actually really like the way he looks. I'm itching to touch that chamois-soft skin again. I'm dying to touch his tail and his horns to see what they feel like. And those obliques... Yeah, his looks aren't the problem.

I think I'm afraid of rejection. I don't say it aloud because it sounds so childish, but it's true. What if I fling myself at him only to find that he thinks humans are ugly and the wrong color and we don't have horns? What if he really is just tolerating me like a sibling and then little sis tries to make out with him?

"I'm dependent on him for safety," I say after a moment. "Without the protection of you guys, I'm doomed to be a slave again. Or worse."

He nods, considering this. "There is a power imbalance, true. Perhaps that's something you should talk with him about."

"I'll think about it," I tell Tarekh. I'm pretty sure I won't say any such thing to Kivian, but I'll sure think about it.

13

KIVIAN

*H*aving a human on board presents a bit of a problem the longer Fran is with us.

I study the four false identification records of the "crew" of the *Dancing Fool*, now temporarily *The Fortune's Fool*. We all have new names, but I'm not entirely sure what to do with Fran. She can't have an official ID, but if we're searched, we need to have some sort of information on her. I eventually decide to mark her down as "cargo" and "pet." I'm sure she's going to give me a mouthful later, and I don't blame her.

It doesn't sit well with me, either.

I wonder if my brother, Jutari, ever has this problem with his mate, Chloe? If others treat her like she's practically an animal instead of a thinking being? It's both perplexing and infuriating. I've learned enough in the small time that I've known Fran to know that her people are not as crude as they're made out to be.

They're experimenting with space travel, for kef's sake. In a few hundred years, maybe a thousand, they'll be ready to join the rest of the universe.

It's not so very long a time. She should be treated like any other sentient being. The unfairness of the situation gnaws at me. We could hide Fran in the cargo bay at security checkpoints, but then we're no better than all the others that treat her like a parcel instead of a person. It's not something that bothered me when my brother introduced his Chloe, and I feel guilty that it took me losing my heart to realize that it's wrong. All of it's really, really wrong. How many humans have I seen on the black market being sold and walked right past because it didn't concern me? How many females have been snatched from everything they know like my Fran and forced into a new, awful world?

She hasn't asked for anything except for me to take her back to Earth...and I refused. Because it's dangerous for *us*. I didn't think about *her*.

Troubled, I push away from my desk and head out of my quarters.

I think about heading to find Fran, but long years as captain force me to tend to duty first. I head to the bridge and to my console, checking our position and the logs of the last few hours. Nothing new. Nothing but quiet. It's almost too quiet. I expected the ooli to come after us long before this. The fact that they haven't gnaws at me. What are they waiting for? I'm sure they have a plan, but I can't figure out what it is. In a way, it's a good thing. The longer we stay hidden in the asteroid belt, the less chance they have of finding us. But the crew's starting to get a little stir-crazy and I don't blame them. Four weeks is a long time to sit, waiting.

I might be the only one that doesn't mind it. Each day that passes is another one I get to spend with Fran. It's nice to be in such a small, confined area like our ship. It means that no matter what we do, we're around each other all day, every day. I never thought it'd be so enjoyable to have another person underfoot, but I look forward to seeing Fran and her smiles, her laughter, even her frowns. They're usually directed at me and something I've said, but I enjoy them anyhow.

She still doesn't know she's my female, though.

It's been difficult to keep my hands to myself, especially with her so close. But when she first came aboard the *Fool*, she'd just been torn from one bad situation and I didn't want to put her into another. I didn't want her to feel like she had to spread her thighs for safety. Just the thought makes me murderous. I've waited, doing my best to be patient and hoping that she'd come to enjoy my teasing and perhaps turn to me at night instead of crawling to the far end of the bed.

It's taken time, but she no longer has that hunted look on her face. She doesn't flinch at the slightest noise and scowl at everyone on the ship. In fact, I think she rather likes my crew.

Me, I'm not sure what she thinks. Sometimes she laughs at my jokes. Sometimes she shakes her head at me as if I'm an idiot that must be tolerated. I flirt with her during sticks. I touch her every opportunity I get.

I even sleep naked next to her.

Fran hasn't noticed. She never reaches out to touch me. She's flirty when I flirt with her, but the moment we leave the sticks table, she puts it away as if it's a game like any other. Sometimes she pays no attention to me at all, not even when I stand so close that my cock responds in painfully obvious fashion.

If she's interested in more than friendship, she hasn't indicated such. So she needs more time.

In a way, I'm rather glad that the star charts continue to show no one in the vicinity. It means more time for us to hide out here amongst the forgotten rocks of space...and more time for Fran to realize that I'm quite the charming fellow.

My mouth twists in amusement at that, picturing Fran's snort of disdain at the thought.

"You seem cheerful," Tarekh comments as he turns around from Alyvos's chair.

I shrug and pretend to look at nav charts when all I can think about is Fran. Fran and her pretty smile and the sensual way she moves. Fran and her soft, soft skin that's such an odd—but enticing—color. "Just in a good mood. Why shouldn't I be?"

"Because it's day thirty-three and no sign of the ooli? I know that's enough to sour Alyvos's mood." He crosses his arms and gazes at me from his seat without getting up. "Myself as well. I don't know if you noticed, but the *Fool's* running in top shape and even that leaky spigot in the mess hall's been fixed. There's absolutely nothing for your mech to do. Or your medic. Or anyone else."

I grin at him. "Shall I cut my finger on my nav panel and let you pat away my sorrows so you have something to do?" I adjust the cuff of one sleeve. "We just can't get blood on my clothes. This shirt's rather new and a favorite of mine."

Tarekh just shakes his head at me. "You're impossible."

"So I'm told." I gesture at the station in front of him. "Alyvos retreating to his bunk?"

"He's tired of staring at the same keffing shit. I know the feeling. About the only entertaining thing to watch on this ship is Fran."

My eyes narrow and I can feel a surge of jealousy rush through me. "Oh?" I try to keep my voice light.

"Calm down," Tarekh says in a lazy voice. "I know better than to eyeball another's mate. It's clear you've decided she's yours. You already announced that to us, remember? This face may be ugly, but the ears hear well enough." He taps one earlobe and then smirks at me. "I'm just curious when you plan on letting her know."

"Not until she's comfortable and feels safe. And not until she indicates she's ready." I give the medic my best playful grin. "Can't exactly announce that she belongs to me moments after I just saved her from slavery, can I? Don't think she'd take that well."

"Didn't stop you before."

"She didn't believe me then. I don't know how she'd react now."

"You're being surprisingly patient," Tarekh admits. "For you."

"I think that's a compliment. I'll take it."

"I must say I'm impressed." A big grin spreads across his rough-hewn face. "Which is why I feel comfortable pointing out to you a conversation I had recently with a certain female."

That wild surge of jealousy rushes through me again. I fight it back, because it's sheer stupidity. Tarekh knows she's mine. She's certainly allowed to talk to him. In fact, it makes me glad she gets along so well with my crew. But the animal instinct that fires up inside my mind can't be calmed. It wants to snarl and demand that no one look at her but me. I pause for a moment to control myself, then ask, "You were talking with Fran? About what?"

"Medical conditions," he says calmly.

I grip the console in front of me with tight hands. "Is she sick?"

"She thought she was. Thought she had a mental condition where she was having feelings for her captor. I talked to her and made her realize that it wasn't an issue. She's allowed to fantasize about people without it being psychological."

I'm astounded. Then jealous again. "Who is she fantasizing about?" Sentorr? She spends a lot of time with him. Alyvos?

"You truly have to ask that?" Tarekh shakes his head at me. "You *are* rather turned around by this female, aren't you?"

"Me?" I can feel the grin spreading across my face. "Now that's good news indeed."

"Thought you might appreciate that."

"What did she say?" I feel like an eager child, waiting for a sweet.

The look on his face is amused. He turns around in his chair and studies his screen for a moment before calling over his shoulder. "Said she had feelings for you and didn't know if they were true ones. She was afraid to act on them. I told her that was wise."

I push out of my chair so quickly that metal scrapes along the floor. "You what?"

He chuckles. "Actually, I don't remember what I told her. But I'm going to give you some advice. You know how to play it smooth when it comes to the ooli or anyone else we're thinking to rob. Might not be a bad idea to play it smooth with her, too."

"Of course I would." I'm indignant at the very thought. Haven't I been patient for weeks now? I've been so patient it's downright obscene.

"Really? You look like an eager young boy about to get his cock wet for the first time."

I scowl at him and run a hand down my face. Sure enough, I'm grinning like the mad fool my ship is named after. He's right in that I should ease off and not charge forward at Fran with my own confession of how much I need her and want her. I'll play it easy and calm, like a game of sticks, where half of the challenge is convincing your opponent you have exactly what you need and know just how to play it.

I can do the same for my lovely Fran.

14

KIVIAN

I find Fran with Alyvos in the cargo bay. They're seated on two crates of the stolen crystals, but the gear spread in front of them is guns, dismantled and pulled apart. As I watch, Alyvos picks up a component of one—a rather dangerous black-matter discharger—and shows it to my mate. "Do you know where this belongs?"

"Not in her hands," I say smoothly, strolling up. "What's going on?"

Fran looks up at me, wiping her hands with a greasy rag. "Alyvos is showing me how to take care of the blasters. He's going to let me check the guns for efficiency and maintain them for you guys." She looks excited at the prospect of handling such a menial chore.

"Thrilling," I say dryly. "He's such a gem to 'allow' you to do this for him."

Alyvos just snaps the discharger into his weapon and shakes his head. "She volunteered. Asked if I had any tasks I felt she could do." He glances up at me. "She's got small hands. Lots of fingers. She'll be good at it."

"It's also dangerous," I point out. "She has to know exactly what she's doing or she could hurt herself."

"Which is why I'm showing her."

I glare at my nav. I don't know why his presence here with her is irritating me so much. Is it that they're sitting close, their knees practically together? Or is it that she went to him instead of coming to me? "I don't know if I like this."

"It's a good thing it's my decision then, isn't it?" Fran says lightly. As I watch, she picks up a scanner and expertly slides it into the shaft of the blaster as if she's been doing this all her life. He's not wrong that she's got the perfect hands for this, but I don't like it. There are too many soldiers missing a finger who got careless while cleaning their blasters.

But instead of teasing her, I retort, "I'm the captain, aren't I?"

Both Fran and Alyvos pause, looking up at me. Fran seems surprised by my terse tone, and Alyvos just smirks. He gets to his feet. "I'll let you two work this out. Fran, come see me when you're ready to continue your lessons."

"Thanks." Her tone is flat and she puts down the components on the crate in front of her, then calmly puts her hands on her knees.

I wait for Alyvos to leave, and then I sit down next to her. "We should talk."

"Oh, we definitely should." She blinks at me, waiting.

"I don't want you doing this."

"I don't want you to have a stick up your ass, but it looks like we're both not going to get what we want."

Her biting retort leaves me speechless, and I stare a moment at her, stunned, before breaking into laughter. It pleases me that a second later, her own shy, slightly wry smile curls her mouth.

"Sorry," she tells me. "I guess that was rude. I don't like being told I can't do something."

"I noticed." I can't help but grin.

"It's not that I'm dying to clean guns, mind you." Fran leans forward and rubs a smudge off of the container in front of her. "I just need something to do to fill my time. I want to be useful. I can't just wander around all day."

"Why not? That's what I do," I tease. "Just wander and let my crew do the work."

She rolls her eyes. "Just because you don't do the same work as the others doesn't mean that you don't work, silly. Even I see that you stay just as busy as everyone else."

I shrug and pick up one of the blasters. It's been completely dismantled, and when I pick up the black-matter cartridge, it feels light. Empty, then. There's no way she could harm herself. I should have given Alyvos more credit. "This isn't a fun task. Alyvos hates doing this sort of thing. Ironic, since he left the military years ago but still acts like he's expecting to go to war at any moment."

"I figured it wasn't fun. That's why I offered to do it. I told him to give me something that he hated doing."

I watch her, curious. "Then why do it?"

"So you'll keep me," Fran says bluntly, looking over at me. "So I'm not just sucking up all your oxygen and you'll feel the need to dump me off at the nearest station."

Does she truly think I would do such a thing? Has she no idea how often I reach over in the bed to caress her, only to pull back at the last minute because I don't want to frighten her? That I'd give anything to touch her, but I don't want her to feel like she's being groped? Perhaps I haven't been clear enough with how I feel. Perhaps I'm hiding it *too* well.

I put my fingers under her chin when she looks away, forcing her to look back at me. "Ah, Fran, my sweet. That's a baseless worry."

"It is?"

"Yes. I'd never dump you at the nearest station. Their docking fees are tremendously expensive."

Her mouth purses and I can't tell if she's going to frown or laugh. Her eyes narrow at me and then she chuckles. "You're joking, right?"

"I am always joking," I say gently. I rub my thumb along the delicate line of her jaw. "I would never dump you to fend for yourself. Have I not told you that you are safe with me?"

"But it's not just you here. It's three other people. I'd like to think that I could have a place here, if I can't have a place anywhere else in the universe."

I don't tell her that most shipping vessels—which is what the *Fool* masquerades as—are four-person crews. I also don't point out that she would never blend in because of her race. I don't want to frighten her. "We'll figure something out."

She gives me a worried look and then nods, pulling out of my grip.

I let my hand fall away and move a little closer to where she sits. "If you want to learn, though, I'm happy to show you how to handle a weapon properly."

Fran seems surprised at my offer. "You will? But you just chased Alyvos off."

"I didn't like how close he was sitting to you," I tell her, and then proceed to sit just as close. Before she can ask, I continue on, "I was always taught that you want to build the gun from the handle on up."

"Oh?"

"Yes." I flash her my most disarming grin. "You want something solid to hold on to. A good grip is priceless."

She arches an eyebrow at me and then flicks her gaze up and down my body. Perhaps she's noticing just how close I'm sitting, then. Or maybe she's noticing that my tail has slid around her bottom and ever so lightly hugs her from behind. I wait for her response, but all she says is, "Do tell."

I'm pretty sure she knows I'm flirting at this point, and I'm also relatively sure she's all right with it. Relatively. Fran is a tricky one to read. "Start with the grip," I tell her, and offer it to her. "If you start with the barrel, you'll be holding it and pointing it at yourself while you put it together. Dangerous. It might go off."

"All over my chest?" she says, her words light and somehow sly.

My heart thunders. Ah, what a female. Is she flirting back? I can't stop the grin on my face—it feels as wide as the asteroid belt we're currently hiding inside. "Yes. Can't have that." I wait for her to hold the handle I've given her. When she takes it, I reach an arm around her shoulders, tucking her against me and correcting her grip, placing my hand over her smaller one. "Hold tight here. It isn't like caressing a lover. The firmer the better."

"Clearly we don't caress our lovers in the same way," she murmurs. "I've always been told a tight grip is the best."

My cock surges at her words. I can't believe she's turning the tables on me. It's the most exciting thing I've ever experienced, and I want to fling her down on these crates and let her show me just how tight her grip is. "Indeed. I suppose it depends on what you're gripping." I lean forward and pick up another piece. "This is a node. There are two of them for this particular blaster. They fit in along the frame like so." I slide one down, then the other. "You want to make sure they're nestled tight, because when the gun fires, it's going to thrust hard." My voice has dropped to a low, husky note. "So you'll need to be ready for that."

Fran's breathing hard. Her long lashes flutter and her gaze is utterly focused on the half-assembled gun in our hands. "I'll be ready."

"Good," I tell her softly. "The biggest piece is the discharger. This is the one that gets the dirtiest and needs the most cleaning. Most people just pay attention to this when it comes to cleaning. They pull off the discharger and make sure it's primed and ready to go and then just continue. Not me."

"No?" She glances up at me, her eyes luminous.

"No," I tell her. "I'm a very thorough male. I like to make sure that everything's as good as I can make it. If that means spending a lot more time with...nodes, then that's what I'll do. A properly handled node can make or break a weapon, you know."

"I didn't know that," she whispers, breathless.

"It's true. It changes everything." I lean in closer. I can smell her hair, floral from the soaps she uses. I can practically touch the shell of her ear with my lips, and I'm dying to move just a little closer and brush my mouth against her skin. "If your node isn't primed, your gun won't fire nearly as accurately. And we want everything to be...perfect."

"We do." Her gaze flicks up to me again. "So you always make sure the node is primed before you...fire?"

"Always," I promise her. "I don't believe in doing things halfway."

She shivers. "No, you don't seem like the type."

"I'm the kind of male that thinks that if you want something done right, you take time with it. And I like to take plenty of time preparing things."

Fran gazes up at me, her lips slightly parted. Her mouth is damp, and I realize she must have licked her lips. I groan low, because I want to be the one licking them. I cup her chin with my fingers again and graze my thumb over that full, sweet mouth.

"Kivian," Tarekh's voice blares over the com, and Fran jerks out of my arms, nearly dropping the half-assembled blaster on the floor. "Guess what."

I clench my jaw as she gets to her feet, my tail flicking against the crates angrily. Blast. Those ooli truly do have the worst timing ever. Jth'Hnai couldn't have planned it any better if he'd tried. I answer Tarekh through clenched teeth. "Let me guess. Our long-lost friend?"

"Yup. We're getting readings on an ooli ship in the belt," Tarekh says, excitement in his voice.

Finally. I look over at Fran, who stands nearby, watching me. She holds the half-assembled blaster in her hands, but her gaze is locked to my face. There's frustration and lust written all over her pretty face.

I get to my feet, take the blaster from her, and assemble it in a matter of seconds, clicking things into place. There's a time for seduction, and this isn't it. "We'll continue this later, my sweet. Until then, perhaps you should retire to my quarters, where it's safe."

15

FRAN

*R*etire to his quarters where it's *safe*?

The man doesn't know me very well, does he? The moment he takes off, I follow him. I kind of expect everyone to be at the bridge of the ship, so I'm surprised to see they're gathering in the hallway next to one of the airlocks. The other three aliens are there, and as I watch, they strap on lightweight chest armor and arm themselves with guns—the very kind I was learning how to clean. Tarekh slides two pistols into holsters on his legs and grabs a wicked-looking club-like instrument, letting it sit on his shoulder like he's waiting for a baseball pitch. Next to him, Alyvos touches something on his gun and it whines to life, a cartridge inside lighting up. Sentorr automatically hands Kivian a gun belt and he straps it on.

They're all swift and efficient, and it's clear this is something they've done dozens—maybe hundreds—of times before.

"Where are you all going?" I ask, when it's clear no one's noticed I'm even there. "What's going on?"

Kivian pauses and gives me a stern look. "Go back to my quarters, Fran. You'll be safe there."

Why am I not safe here? I frown and don't move, looking to the others for an answer.

It comes from stiff, no-nonsense Sentorr. "The ooli have located us. They'll be looking to reclaim their cargo. We plan on stopping them."

I gasp, a cold rush of fear moving through me. "They're boarding us?"

Tarekh laughs. "More like we're going to board *them*."

Oh. Er. "Is that dangerous?'

"Oh yes." His eyes gleam with excitement.

Definitely something they've done before. "You're all going? Who's going to pilot the ship?" AKA, what about me? The lone person staying behind? I look at Kivian, worried.

He finishes adjusting his gun belt and checks one last cartridge on his guns before turning to me. He moves forward and grasps my arms gently, steering me aside. I realize a moment later he's blocking out the others with his body even as he moves closer to me and runs a finger along my jaw. "I promise you'll be safe, little one. The ooli are terrible fighters. This won't take long. The *Fool's* on autopilot. She's going to wait a few hours, and then if anything bad happens, she's set to fly to the nearest station with an emergency signal. You'll be all right."

"Yeah, you say I'll be all right, but you guys are packing some serious heat." I gesture at the now-full gun belt he's got around his waist. "I don't want you to get hurt," I whisper. "Can you just call this whole thing off?"

He shakes his head, a slow grin spreading across his face. I'm pretty sure I'm blushing with embarrassment at what I just said. "I don't want you to get hurt" might as well be me stamping I HAVE A CRUSH on my forehead. I'll worry about that later, though.

"I vow you're safe here on the *Fool*, Fran," he says in a low voice. "I won't let them get to you. You're mine now."

Awareness prickles through my body. That's not the first time he's said such a thing, and I wonder what exactly he means by it. I don't get a creepy feeling from him like I did the frog-guys. If anything, I feel...excited at what it could mean. "This isn't the time for flirting," I tell him. Of course, when I say it like that, it sounds just like even more flirting. God, I'm so hopeless.

"Think of it as more of a promise."

"Do you have to go?" I bite my lip, because I know that sounds selfish, but I can't help it. What if they all die and leave me here alone on this ship? That's not my only worry, of course. I picture Kivian getting hurt and I feel like I'm going to throw up.

"I won't put my men in danger and stay behind," he tells me. He strokes my jaw again, making it difficult for me to concentrate on what he's saying. "Don't worry about me, though, sweet Fran. I may not have had a chance to show you how good I am with a weapon, but my aim is true." He winks. "I'll give you a private lesson when I get back."

"You're seriously the most incorrigible man I've ever met," I tell him, but I'm smiling. "So, what, you're going to go over there and just kill yourself a bunch of froggies?"

"Kill them?" Kivian gives me a surprised look. "While I admit that's an easy way out, it's not my style. No, we're just going to rob them of whatever crystal they have left, wipe any trace of the *Fool* from their records, and put the crew in stasis. Alyvos can set their ship to pilot them back to a safe place..." He grins. "In a good year or two. By then we'll be long gone and so will the crystal. They can't report it stolen because it's contraband." He chucks my chin. "Much like you, my sweet."

I swat his hand away. "So what, I sit here and wait like the little wifey? I'd rather go with you. I can help. I can fire a gun." Once someone shows me how. I gesture at Tarekh's bat-like club. "Or give me one of those. I can use that."

"You're half the size of them, and I won't risk the chance of one of the ooli touching you ever again." His jaw grows firm. "You stay here."

"Are you two going to talk all day or can we board already? We've already locked our ship to theirs." Sentorr calls. "If we wait much longer they're going to be trying to board us and not the other way around."

Kivian grins and caresses my cheek. "Go to my rooms," he insists, and then turns and joins his crew, pulling out his blaster. There's a big smile on his face. "I'm ready. Let's go say hello."

Alyvos and the others shoot me a look, but then they march into the next chamber, the door sealing behind them. Something flashes on screen and the computer chirps out something in an alien language. I wish I still had that annoying translator bulb in my ear, because I want to know what it's saying.

I'm here alone. Well, shit. I cross my arms and stare at the sealed portal they disappeared through, willing Kivian or someone else to return. No one does, though, and I decide I'm not going to Kivian's chambers to wait. I sit down on the floor where I'm at. I'm going to wait right here.

I get up two seconds later, because I decide I need a weapon.

Then I'm going to wait right here.

I find a really ugly, long-looking thing that I can only assume is a vase perched on one of Kivian's fussy-looking tables. Funny how a man that's so overwhelmingly masculine can have such odd taste in furniture and clothing. It feels heavy, though, and solid, like it's made of metal. I heft it and head over to the hatch, waiting. I can't hear anything on the other side, which is frustrating. I press my ear to the door and there's noise, all right, but not the sound of fighting or guns blasting or anything recognizable. It's just...noise.

I don't know what to do. I clutch my vase, terrified. They said they had it under control, but how long do things like this take? What if they're in trouble and I'm just sitting here, holding table decorations when they could need my help?

What if Kivian needs me?

I swallow hard, an enormous knot in my throat. Worry gnaws at me, and when there's a loud groan of metal and the *Fool* shifts, I panic. I don't want to be here in space alone. I don't want to be left behind if the others are dead.

I don't want to be without Kivian.

The realization strikes me with the force of a hammer. I don't have just a crush on him. I'm in love with the big idiot, ridiculous shirts and all. I love his laugh and the way his eyes gleam when he's challenged. I love the way he looks at me just before we go to sleep. Being abandoned in space hasn't been all that bad... because he's been at my side every step of the way.

If I don't have him...I don't have anything. I wouldn't trade his safety for a one-way trip back to Earth.

I gnaw on a fingernail, quietly freaking out. "Um, computer?" I call, curious to see if it'll answer me, even though I'm speaking English. "Are you there?"

"What is your query?" the smooth, unnatural voice asks me.

"Um, I need to know if Kivian and the others are okay on the other side."

"Please define your parameters more clearly," it tells me. "Parameters that require clarification due to language barrier: 'others,' 'okay,' and 'other side.'"

Oh, fuck me. "How many life forms do you show aboard the fucking—excuse me, *keffing*—enemy ship?"

That gets a response. "Sensors indicate four life forms."

Four?!

Only *four*?

A panicked sob catches in my throat. Four? That might mean it's a fight to the death and the others need my help to survive… depending on if any of them are left. I imagine Kivian on the other side of the door, reaching for me, unable to quite get to the release that would open the hatch…and me standing stupidly on the other side with a vase, waiting.

Waiting.

Waiting.

Screw that. I've never been the kind of girl that's good at waiting. Just look at how bad I am at sticks. *Patience is not one of your virtues*, I tell Duh Fran. *Why wait until it's too late?*

It's enough to convince me.

"Computer," I bellow out. "I need you to open this fricking door because I'm coming through."

"Please define your parameters more clearly," it begins.

Argh!

To my surprise, a moment later, the door hatch hisses and begins to open. Oh god. What if I'm too late? What if it's the enemy deciding to come through on this side? I clutch my vase tight, ready to attack.

A figure pushes forward, and before I can think, I swing. The vase hammers into the midsection of the alien in front of me, nearly snapping my wrists with the impact.

Kivian doubles over, groaning. He looks up at me in shock. "Fran? Wh-what's wrong?" he wheezes.

"Nothing!" I tell him.

And then I burst into noisy tears.

16

KIVIAN

"So, you got all of the crystal?" Fran's eyes are still reddened from her weeping fit earlier, making me feel guilty despite the beaming smile on her face. I rub my stomach, not sure if I'm more upset that I'm going to have a sore gut for the next day, or that Fran was so terrified she felt she had to attack.

It's the latter, of course. I hate that my mate was so frightened. "The crystal's unimportant," I say, and gesture that she should come sit by me on my bed.

We're in my quarters. I needed to bathe after working up a sweat in the ooli ship, since they keep the temperature at a swampy heat that made me swim in my own juices moments after we boarded. Fran followed me in, still rattled. The others are in the mess hall, celebrating our victory and the crystal we've brought on board, as well as all of the other plunder we took while on board. We should join them, but I think Fran needs a few minutes to herself to gather her thoughts…and I just need to be around her.

I've never felt such fear until she rammed me in the gut with a priceless Ilsi vase. Not over the vase—though I like to think of it as a retirement plan of sorts—but the fact that she was so terrified. I immediately thought she was in danger, and I've never felt such intense terror. Such intense need to protect another person. She's become everything to me so very quickly.

Even thinking about her in danger still has me rattled. Truth be told, she wasn't even at risk. The situation was handled. And yet…

We can't go on like this.

We got the crystal from the ooli. That much is true. We cleaned out their stores and emptied their stash of credits into our own coffers. I tell myself that's what they get for dealing with contraband. Truth is, I don't feel bad in the slightest for stealing from them. Physical credit chits are only used to buy illegal things, like banned technology, crystals…

And slaves.

Along with trunks full of chits, two cases of crystals and enough wine and weapons to make me wonder what kind of party these ooli were going to throw, we also retrieved their ship's logs. Included in those logs are the usual chatter…and several communications between Jth'Hnai and an unnamed trader. The ooli had lamented to him about his toy being stolen from him on Haal Ui Station and wanted a replacement. The trader agreed and made an agreement to meet up on a nearby station—a seedy one—so Jth'Hnai could pick out a new plaything, free of charge for being such a good customer.

A few months ago, I would have taken that information and robbed both the ooli when they showed up and the slaver of his credits and been on my way. Now, I can't stop thinking about the human females that are being held captive even now. Are they strong and brave like my Fran? Or terrified?

I can't leave them to their fate, no more than I can leave Fran to hers.

She's not mesakkah. To our race and dozens of others, she's nothing but a walking, talking toy. A pet. She knows nothing about our world or any of the other cultures that populate the galaxy.

All she's ever asked for is to go home.

A month ago, I'd said no. Said I couldn't ask that of my crew. Now, everything's changed. Fran holds my heart in her delicate hands and I can't bear the thought of not being able to protect her. She'll be safest on Earth, away from all of this.

I'll take her back to her home planet. It's a long, dangerous journey, but she deserves happiness and a long life. As a pirate's captive toy, I don't know that she'll have either. The thought makes me ache, but I can't sacrifice my contentment for hers.

I want to immediately vid my brother and ask him how he keeps Chloe safe. How he handles the stress of having such a person as his mate, but I know the answer—he's chosen to live as a farmer on some backwater planet where no one ever goes, because he can't give her up. My brother, who was once one of the most feared mercenaries in six galaxies, grows crops and digs in the dirt...all for the love of a female.

Would I do the same?

"I would, but I'm a terrible farmer," I murmur.

"What?" Fran gives me a curious look, sniffing.

I pat the bed again. "Come sit." I want to demand it, not ask, but I know my Fran. I also know I need to touch her, if nothing else than to reassure myself that she's all right. Her fear is gnawing at my soul.

Fran moves cautiously forward, her eyes luminous, and she sits next to me. Her gaze is locked on mine and she looks so fragile and lonely that it hurts me.

I know I shouldn't, but I can't help myself—I haul her into my lap, tucking her under my chin and holding her close. She stiffens in my arms for a brief moment, and then yields when she realizes I'm not going to attack her.

"Are you all right, little one?" I murmur against her soft hair. "Shall we talk about why you're so upset?"

She relaxes against me for a long moment, silent, and then punches my shoulder with one small fist. "You assholes left me *behind.*"

I want to laugh, except she's truly upset. "It was for your safety, I promise."

"Really? What am I supposed to do if something happens to you?"

I shake my head. "It was an easy fight. Once we boarded, the ooli ran and hid from us. No one fired a single shot. All we did was round them up and sent them into cryo-sleep. It's one of the easiest takeovers I've ever had." It was so easy, it was practically laughable. I suspect she would have enjoyed it, if she'd have been there. She would have liked to see the outraged look on Jth'Hnai's ugly face when he realized it was us boarding his ship to rob him a second time. Ah, that was a good moment.

"The computer told me it only saw four life signs." Her voice is hard. Flat. Accusing.

Is that why she was so panicked? "Mm. Yes, when there are people in cryo-sleep, most systems don't count those as technically 'alive.' You are but you aren't, and so it likely only picked up our signals."

Her jaw clenches with mutinous anger, but she nods, understanding.

I'm still surprised at her frustration. "You're angry," I say, wonderingly, and touch a finger to her jaw. "Why?"

To my surprise, her mouth begins to tremble. "You left me." Her voice is hoarse with emotion. "What am I supposed to do if something happens to *you*?"

She's already said that once, but her emphasis changes everything. My heart pounds and my body aches with what could have been. I know what I have to do, though. She can't stay here with us. She's right—if anything were to happen to me, she's a target for every deviant male on this side of the universe. "My sweet Fran," I murmur, stroking her cheek. "I haven't been fair to you."

"No, you haven't," she murmurs, her gaze on my mouth. "You should have let me come with you."

I don't know whether to laugh or groan in agony. The heated looks she's sending my way are the most delicious torture possible. She shifts on my lap and her thigh rubs against my aching cock in the most incredible—and frustrating—way. If only I'd pushed harder, taken her when I had the chance—

But then it would be that much more difficult to let her go, and let her go I must. Keffing hell, but I hate having to be virtuous. It's not a trait that suits me well. "I wouldn't risk you, little one."

"You're not risking me," she tells me in a soft, soft voice. Her arms go around my neck and she moves closer to me. I'm helpless to resist the lure of her words, her sweet lips, her nearness. "I'm the one that's 'risking' me."

"I won't let you—"

She puts a finger to my lips, stopping my words. "You don't get to decide," she whispers, and leans in to press her mouth to mine.

I'm so fascinated by this strange movement that I forget all hygiene laws and remain utterly still as her lips brush against mine. I'm not revolted—in fact, I'm more aroused than I think I've ever been before, and I groan. Her breath fans against my skin and I feel the tip of her tongue slide along the seam of my mouth. She pulls away a moment later, a hint of a smile on her face as she meets my gaze. "Do your people not kiss?"

"Is that what this is, then?" She's mentioned it before. No wonder she stared so hard at my mouth just now. I can't stop gazing at hers. It's shiny and her lips are so fascinatingly plump. It makes me want to do that all over again.

Fran nods and rubs up against my chest, her mouth close to mine, so close that our breath is mingling. "Want me to show you how to do it?"

I shouldn't. I should be virtuous and push her away—again, not one of my better qualities. Instead of telling her no, I groan and cup the back of her neck, leaning in and pushing my mouth against hers.

It doesn't feel quite the same when I do it—my lips mash too enthusiastically against hers and she goes still against me, waiting. I feel like a callow youth that's never gotten his cock wet, and I inwardly command myself to do better. She was gentle when she caressed me, and I can't help but think that I should follow that lead. I soften my mouth, caressing her lips with mine in soft, exploratory nibbles.

That elicits a moan from her, one so throaty and achingly gorgeous that the hairs on the back of my neck stand up...along with my cock. Ah, she's sweet, my Fran. Her lips are marvelous, and I can't stop kissing them. Such a deviant sort of hobby, this kissing. No wonder people keep snatching humans to take as slaves—

I jerk away from her, hating my own thoughts. Slaves.

She gazes up at me with confused eyes. "What's wrong?"

"We can't do this," I tell her, caressing her cheek with my thumb. "It's not right."

"What's not right about it? We haven't even gotten to the tongues yet."

Tongues? Have mercy. I've never been so keffing hard. I close my eyes, trying to stay in control of my body. Her fingers play against my nape, and I can feel the swell of her large, bouncy breasts pushing against my chest, can feel the slight weight of her hips on my thigh. Why is everything about her so perfect?

I bury my face against her neck, inhaling her scent. I can't resist a little lick of her skin there. Another hygiene law broken, but I'm not sure I care. Judging from her gasp and the way her fingers tighten against me, she doesn't care either.

But that's all I'll allow myself. Reluctantly, I pull back. I can feel the throb of need from my horns to my tail, but I can't give in to it. It's not fair to her. "We need to talk, Fran."

Her dark eyes widen and she gives me a worried glance. "You know, when humans say that kind of thing, it's never good."

"This is good, I promise." I pull one of her hands from my shoulder and clasp it in my own, against my chest. "Remember how you said you wanted to go home? Back to your planet?"

She tilts her head and gives me a narrow-eyed look. "Don't."

I ignore that little statement and continue. "On the ooli ship, we pulled their records. They were going to pick up another human slave for Jth'Hnai. The trader he was in communication with mentioned him picking his choice, which means he has several. I know the others aren't keen on traveling to Earth, but with the money we've made off of these shipments, we'll have more than enough to go off the maps for a bit and take the scenic route back to your galaxy—"

"No."

"—Along with a few friends we pick up along the way. We'll rescue the others and bring you all back to Earth—"

"No." Her expression gets even more stubborn.

"—And it'll be a good deed for all and we can return to our lives, knowing that those ooli won't be touching another human female. I think it's a very good plan, don't you?"

"No," she repeats firmly. She looks furious, but her lower lip trembles. "Is that what you want, then? You want to go back to your regular life without me around?"

17

KIVIAN

I've hurt her. Kef it, why do I have to be the noble one? I'm terrible at it. "Truth be told, I'd rather have you naked and in my bed under me, breaking every hygiene law from here to my Homeworld."

Her eyes widen with surprise. "You would?"

"More than anything." My voice is husky with emotion. "Don't make it harder for me to be noble than it already is."

She gives a little laugh that sounds like a half-sob. "I don't want you to be noble, you big bastard. I like the laughing, cheating Kivian that doesn't give a damn about the rules. I don't want to go back to Earth—not if you're not there."

I groan. "You're not making this easy."

"I don't want it to be easy! I want to stay with you." She cups my jaw in her small hands, her earnest gaze searching my face. "You big idiot, I've fallen in love with you and I don't want to leave you behind. I don't want you to leave me behind, either. I want to learn how to be useful in your crew. I want to wake up in your arms instead of just in your bed. I want to break all those hygiene laws *with* you."

"Fran, little one. I would love nothing more than that. But every day that you're out here with me, you're not safe."

"Why?"

"What do you mean, *why*?"

"Just that." She shrugs. "Why am I not safe?"

"Well, for one, this is a pirate ship with no plans for retirement. We make our living smuggling and stealing."

"So?"

"So we're wanted in several galaxies, and if the law ever gets their hands on us, we'll be spending the rest of our lives on the most remote prison planets they can find."

"Then we don't let them find us. You'd really let someone take you off to prison?" She arches an eyebrow at me. "That doesn't sound like you."

"No, most likely we'd go down fighting."

"I'd do the same. And I trust you to keep us out of the law's hands." She pats my chest, as if that's answered all her questions. "You're not new at this, I can tell. How long have you been a pirate?"

I shrug. "Thirty years, give or take."

She sputters. "We're going to have the racial age discussion some other time. For now, I think it's safe to say that if we get another thirty years out of this, we'll be doing great. Most marriages don't last half as long." Her fingers trace along my jaw and slide down my neck in the most erotic—and ticklish—of touches. "Is that the only concern? It doesn't matter to me. I know what I'm getting into."

Why is she making this sound so very simple? "It's not my only concern. There's the fact that you're a contraband race—"

"All the more reason not to get caught with me." She gives me an impish look and licks her lips.

Those damned, glorious lips. I want to taste them again. "It's not me I'm worried about, Fran. It's others that think of you as a pet or a slave."

"You'll protect me," she whispers, leaning forward. The tips of her breasts graze against the plates on my chest, and I feel the erotic contact all through my body. Her tempting mouth is dangerously close to mine again. "And you can show me how to protect myself. Show me how to shoot a gun. How to take care of myself. How to be part of your crew."

I don't point out that most vessels of this class are four-person jobs. Truth be told, there's room for her in my cabin, and the others don't mind her coming along. There's always more to be done, and I'd love to have her at my side. Not just because I'm dying to taste her lips again, or to push my cock into the wet heat of her cunt—I love her mind. I love that she's brave enough to try to prick my ego when it gets too big, and that she's not afraid of telling me her thoughts. I love that throaty, gleeful laugh she makes when I let her win at sticks.

She's my mate. I must be an idiot to even consider letting her go.

"What about Earth?" I ask, because I have to.

"What about your planet?" she challenges. "If I stay with you, I want to be your partner. Not your pet. I'm pretty sure that means we won't be accepted back in your home town."

"No civilized planet will have me anymore," I tell her with a grin.

"Then we'll just have to stick to uncivilized ones." Fran leans in and brushes her lips against mine in the briefest of caresses, and my cock feels like steel. "And be uncivilized together. If that's what you want." She leans back, a worried look on her face. "You...haven't said what you want."

"Didn't I? I'm pretty sure I mentioned you in my bed." I slide a hand down to caress the rounded curve of her glorious bottom.

"Yes, but I'm just yammering on with plans and you're just agreeing with me. I don't want that. We have to both want the same thing. If you don't want me here, just say so." She looks troubled and so very miserable.

How can she not think that I want her?

Perhaps it's time I show her, instead.

I cup her face in my hands, gaze into her eyes, and then press my mouth to hers. "I want you," I tell her between quick, short kisses. "I want you naked against me. I want your skin to mine. I want to touch you without plas-film or anything else between us. I want to violate every hygiene law possible. I want to push my cock into you and watch you cry out with pleasure. I want..." I hesitate, and then decide to plunge forward. "I want to fill you with my child."

Her eyes go wide with surprise at my words. "You...you mean that? All of that?"

"I do." I kiss her again, brushing my lips over hers. I'm addicted to that small touch and I plan on doing it repeatedly every day for the rest of our lives. "And if you want me to give up piracy...I suppose I can try to find something else to do." I think of Jutari on his farm and I get it, I really do. Maybe he'd need help growing crops. I shudder at the thought, but if it would make Fran happy, then it would make me happy.

"Who said anything about giving up your job?" She frowns at me, caressing my face. "I want to stay with you here on the *Fool*. I want to be a pirate with you."

"I'm not putting you in danger," I warn.

"It's not about what you want. It's about what I want." She gets a mischievous look in her eyes. "And if you won't let me be a pirate, I guess I'll have to be...pirate's booty." She shifts on my lap, pressing her bottom against me.

I groan. "What are you talking about?"

"Just an Earth thing. Ignore me." She presses her mouth to mine again and her tongue slicks against the seam of my lips. "Can we just vow to love each other and kiss now?"

"We can."

With that, my sweet Fran kisses me like she wants to devour me. Her tongue brushes against my lips again, and I recall what she said about using tongues. Is she...wanting to rub her tongue against mine? The thought makes me groan low in my throat. I don't think I've ever wanted anything so much. I feel hers flick against the seam of my mouth and I part my lips to let her in.

The smooth, slick heat of her tongue brushes against mine and need cascades through me. It's the most erotic thing, and I can't help but respond to her caress. I use my tongue like she does hers, dancing with little light touches along the other, exploring and tasting. Time seems to slow as she rubs her tongue along mine, and I feel it right down to my cock, as if she's licking my spur.

There's another deviant thought that I like very much.

When we break from the kiss, she's panting as hard as I am, and her eyes are glazed with need. "You...your tongue has ripples."

"Yours doesn't," I reply, nipping at her lower lip. I'm already addicted to this "kissing." I need more.

"That's so odd," she breathes. "Good, but odd." She moves a hand and traces my brow and the ridges there. "Are you rippled everywhere? You know I have to ask."

"If you mean my cock, the answer is yes. Humans are smooth, I take it?" The shocked look on her face tells me everything, and I grin. "Ah, discovering all the ways we are different is going to be such a pleasure, my sweet mate."

"Oh boy," she whispers. "You aren't kidding."

I lean in and kiss her again, and as I do, I pull on one of the sleeve ties to the oversized shirt she's wearing. "I know we'll have to get you some appropriately sized clothing when we head back to civilization, but I confess I like seeing you wearing my shirts. It makes me think about stripping them off of you and getting you naked under me."

With an expert tug, the sleeve falls away, revealing her bare arm. I stroke her soft skin lightly, fascinated by the feel of her. She pulls on her belt-cord, loosening it and then tossing it aside, and by the time her other sleeve is undone, I can pull the entire thing over her head. I study her face to make sure there's no misgivings or worry there, but all I see is need. Even so, I want it to be her idea, so I kiss her and wait.

Fran makes an impatient sound against my mouth and then pulls away, yanking her shirt—my shirt—over her head and tossing it to the floor. Normally I would protest about such rough care for my clothing, but she's naked in my arms and my shirt's the last thing I give a kef about.

All that smooth skin is bared before me and I can't resist touching her. I stroke my hand up one thigh, watching her face as I do so.

"So," she says, all breathless. "Do I need to show you a few things since I'm your first to touch?"

I grin at the cocky confidence in her words. "Little one, I've touched females before, just not skin to skin. Not like this." I glide my hand up her thigh, towards her heat. "This is much, much better."

"I don't want to hear about other females."

"Good, because I can't even think about them. No one existed before you. All I can think of is Fran and only Fran." The only thing on my mind is touching Fran. Teasing her. Making her come.

"That's just how I like it," she says playfully, and puts her arms around my neck. She leans in and kisses my jaw, avoiding the sweep of my horns. "Can I taste you everywhere I want to?"

I groan. "Gods, yes."

As she nibbles on my skin, making my cock ache, I let my hand slide up to the vee of her cunt. What I thought was just shadow turns out to be a fascinating little tuft of hair between her thighs. "Why, hello, what's this?" I murmur. "A surprise? I love surprises."

I love the little gasp she makes when I touch her there. "Are you... do you not have hair there?"

"I do not. Though now I'm hurt that you never looked," I tell her with a teasing laugh. "Here I was getting naked and parading around in the hopes of enticing your attention."

"We were supposed to be just friends," Fran says. "I was doing my best to be your friend. That means no looking."

"I prefer us like this."

"Me, too." Her gaze flicks to my mouth, and just that little glance makes me growl fiercely. I pull her closer and capture her mouth with mine, exploring her with kisses even as I discover if her cunt is the same as any other or if it's as charmingly unique as my Fran.

My fingers glide over her folds, and she's soft and wet and scorching hot. It's never felt like this before. I've never touched skin-to-skin, and the sensation is as erotic as it is addictive. My skin slicks along hers and I can feel the little shivers she makes as I explore her. I caress her folds as I kiss her, and my need for her feels like it's growing with every moment that passes. I've never been so aroused by touching a female.

But this is Fran. Of course she's better in every single way. She's the one I've been waiting for.

As I touch her, my fingers rub over a small bump of flesh near the top of her cleft, and Fran jolts in my arms, making a surprised noise of pleasure. She grabs my wrist and moans, her eyes closing.

What...was that?

I freeze, because it seems that human anatomy has a few surprises. "Did I hurt you?"

"No," she breathes, and she's panting hard. She's not pushing my hand away, I notice, just gripping it tight. "Do...do your blue women not have a clit?"

"Is that what this is?" I brush my fingertips up and down her slick valley once more, looking for it. Sure enough, the moment

I rub over her "clit" again her entire body trembles against mine.

"Very. Sensitive," she tells me, gasping. Her other hand has latched tight around the back of my neck and I can feel her muscles clenching.

Fascinating. "Well, now. Should I stop?"

"Noooo."

I chuckle at the utter sorrow in her response. "My poor, sweet little human. I promise I can stop touching you there. Just tell me if it's too much."

My "sweet" little human grabs one of my horns and holds tight. "If you stop I'll never speak to you again."

"Well now, I can't have that, can I?" Very lightly, I rub up against that pleasure spot, and I'm delighted when she closes her eyes and cries out. It seems that I've found a magical little button that makes my Fran light up.

Oh, this is going to be endless amounts of *fun*, I can tell already.

I stroke her over and over, watching her reactions, learning her body. She likes it best when I'm gentle and light with touches, and when I'm too brisk, she doesn't seem to respond. Teasing the hood of flesh encircling the little nub seems to get the best reaction, and she's practically crawling out of her skin and climbing me as I pet her.

I don't stop even when she's keening and moaning my name, or when her hand grips my wrist so tight I'm surprised at her strength. She's not pushing me away, after all. She's just desperately trying to anchor herself to something, and I can guess why.

Seconds later, she lets out a surprised sob and I can feel her entire body clench up in response. She calls my name and her thighs grip my hand tightly, trembling, even as I feel her grow wetter and wetter.

I'm utterly fascinated, and if I wasn't already in love with her, I would be now. I love that she's trapped my hand against her cunt, as if it's too much but she's still not willing to let me go. So I keep rubbing her clit, because I'm a sadistic son of a bitch and I want to see if I can make that happen again. I've never seen a female so responsive, so lost in the moment.

And she's *mine*.

I rub her little clit until she's clenching around my hand again. This time, she pushes me away, gasping, and I remove my hand. I'm fascinated by just how wet it is—all from her body—and I can't resist a taste. I bring my fingers to my mouth and lick her juices off of them. It's musky and delicious and I need more.

"Kivian," she pants, clinging to me as I suck the sweetness of her off of my skin. "You're bound and determined to break all of those laws, aren't you?"

"I've never been much of a rule-follower," I tell her thickly. "Lie back so I can taste you again, little one."

"No," she tells me, startling me. Fran meets my gaze with dark, liquid eyes that seem to devour me. "I want to taste *you* first."

Ah, how can a male refuse such a request? "I'm all yours, little one."

She beams a smile at me and gets off of my lap, getting to her knees on the bed beside me. She tugs at my clothing and then frowns when it doesn't seem to be moving no matter how many knots she unties. "Um. You might want to get rid of the first layer for me."

I chuckle and get to my feet. "As my female wishes." I think for a moment about taking my time and teasing her, but I'm no fool—I want her hot, fascinating mouth on me, tasting me just like she promised. So I quickly remove my shirt and then my trou, kicking them aside before standing before her in my naked glory.

Her eyes are wide as she stares at my cock, and for a moment, I feel a bit of doubt. "Your males...they have cocks, do they not?"

"Not like that," she murmurs, unable to look away from my groin.

I glance down at my equipment, but it all looks normal to me. "Which part? I'm not furry like you." I cup my sac, as if demonstrating to her.

"Oh my god, never say 'furry' again," she tells me and then extends a hand, indicating I should come forward. "Kivian, I love you, but your dick kind of worries me."

"It does? Why?" I step forward so she can do with me as she pleases, though I'm growing more concerned by the minute. I want my Fran to be excited to touch me, not alarmed.

Her hands slide around to my ass and she caresses my skin, and I momentarily forget all about her worry as the feel of her hands gliding over my muscles sends a rush of pleasure through my body. I groan, closing my eyes.

"You're so...big," she murmurs.

"Flattery," I tell her thickly. "Of course I'm big. I'm much taller than you. I would imagine we should still fit, though."

"That's not the part that worries me." She leans in closer and her hand moves to the front of my thigh, as if she's going to touch me...but still doesn't. "What's this part here?" Her fingers lightly stroke my spur.

I nearly collapse at that small touch. I was definitely not prepared for how good her hand would feel there. "It's a spur? Your males don't have one?"

"What's it for?"

"Nothing, I imagine. It's just there, like my tail. Maybe it had a use in the past, but now it's just here to frighten sweet human females away from putting their mouths on mesakkah males."

"Oh, I'm not frightened away." Fran gives me a challenging look. "I just want to make sure there are no hidden spikes or anything."

"No spikes," I tell her thickly. "No hidden anything. I promise." Her breath is fanning against my cock and my belly, and I'm having a hard time concentrating. Closer, I want to tell her. Move closer. But she has to do it on her own terms.

"Just a big thick blue cock with all these ridges, right?" Her voice is so soft and sultry that it makes my sac tighten in response. I want to bury my hand in her hair when she curls her fingers around my length, testing it. "Well, big thick cock and spur, of course."

"The spur won't harm you."

"I know you won't hurt me," she tells me, and looks up at me with the most playful smile on her mouth. "It's just startling to see. Is it sensitive?"

"Not really," I begin, but then she runs her finger lightly underneath it and my knees get weak. "Maybe...maybe a little."

Fran chuckles and pats the bed. "Do you need to lie down while I touch you?"

"No. I'm fine." I hope. Plus, from this angle, I get to watch her kneel down in front of me. It's like every dream I've had come to life, and I wonder if I shouldn't pinch myself to make sure I'm awake.

But then she lowers her head and her tongue slides over the crown of my cock, and there's no denying that this is real. Nothing in my mind compares to how that just felt. "Ah, Fran…"

"Let me know if I do anything you don't like," she murmurs, and kisses the head.

"I like all of it," I reassure her, flexing my hands so I don't grab her hair and push her mouth down on my cock. "Do with me as you like."

She glances up at me through her lashes and gives me a coy little smile even as she runs the tip of her tongue over my cock.

I groan, and now I'm panting as hard as she was. I watch, utterly fascinated, as she sucks on the head of my cock and then takes me deeper into her mouth, rubbing my length along her tongue as she pulls me deep. My cock's fucking her lovely, soft mouth, and the feeling of my bare skin against her lips is better than I could have ever imagined.

I'm pretty sure this violates so many laws that I'd be wanted in six systems. I'm also pretty sure I don't care. I'd give up anything and everything for just a few more moments of Fran's mouth on me. When she makes a little sound of pleasure as she sucks on me, I can feel it all through my body, and I wrap my tail around her arm, desperate to anchor her to me in any way I can.

My female. My Fran.

She's perfect.

I reach down and caress her cheek as she licks my cock, over and over again. Her gaze is locked on me, and I've never seen any creature more beautiful. Did I think humans were strange looking? Clearly I was mad, because I love Fran's smooth little brow and her delicate features. I love her five fingers and her lack of a tail. I love her skin that's the strange shade of a fruit I saw in a marketplace once. I love everything about her and most of all, I love that she's mine.

One of her hands goes to my spur and she caresses it, sending electric flashes of pleasure up my spine. I stiffen, about to lose control, and then pull away from her. "No, my sweet," I rasp, even though every urge I have is telling me to pump into the hot well of her mouth until I spill. But not this time. Not for our first time together. I want to bury myself inside her and gaze down at her lovely face as I make her mine. "I want to come inside you when I release. I'm too close as it is."

She nods, eyes dark with need, and when I get down on the bed next to her, she wraps her arms around my neck and leans in for another kiss. She's as addicted to them as I am. Being naked with her offers a new kind of pleasure, though—the heat of her skin against mine as her breasts push against my chest plating. I flick my tongue against hers in light, flirty caresses, even as I run my hands up and down her bottom, squeezing it. So soft. So keffing soft.

I'm ruined for her. Nothing will ever taste as good, be as soft, or smell as sweet as my Fran does.

I squeeze her thigh and then pull her against me, using my tail to brush a lock of hair out of her face. "Are you ready for your mate, little one?"

She bites her lip and nods at me. "I love you, Kivian."

Her soft words fill me with a fierce pleasure. "I love you too, my Fran. I'm only sorry I didn't tell you how I felt earlier, because then we could have spent the last three weeks making love instead of playing sticks." I lean in and nip at the dusky tip of one of her breasts. Such lovely, rounded little mounds.

Fran chuckles, running her hand up and down my arm and then

squeezing my bicep. "Just consider it a lot of foreplay. Besides, we have all the time in the world to make love."

"Mmm." I drag my tongue over her nipple and love the way she shivers. "I might have to break something just so we can remain out here another week and I can keep you in my bed."

"I think that's an excellent idea," she tells me, breathless and squirming underneath me.

I move up to kiss her again, and she hooks a foot around my hip, parting her legs for me. I twine my tail around her ankle, holding her in place, and push her other thigh wide so I can settle in between them. She moans, eager with anticipation, her hands fluttering over my chest and arms as if she's not sure where to touch me. I take one of her hands in mine and bear it down to the bed. I use my other hand to fit the head of my cock at the entrance to her core.

I can *feel* how wet she is. It's incredible. She's incredible.

"Kivian," she breathes, as I slowly push into her, and our eyes lock.

"I'm ruined," I whisper to her. "You've ruined me."

Nothing else could feel so amazing. So intense. So...deeply connected. It's like we're one being, and when I slowly surge into her, I can see—and feel—everything about her. I'm fascinated by the way her lips part ever so slightly. The way her lashes flutter each time I thrust into her. The way her nipples graze against my chest when I lean in.

It takes a few shallow thrusts for me to fully seat myself into her. I want to go slow, make sure her body can take all of me. Her cunt is an intensely tight grip that's utterly stunning to experience.

The moment I thrust fully into her, though, she gasps in shock, and her heel digs into my hip, her eyes wide.

"What?" I ask, going still. "What is it?" Did I somehow hurt her? The thought makes me sick.

"Spur," she breathes.

Spur?

I reach between our bodies, and sure enough, my spur taps against the little node of her clit when I'm pushed deep inside her. "It hurts?"

"God, no," Fran tells me. "It feels incredible."

I laugh with sheer joy. "You just aged me three years, little one."

"So, what, that makes you nine hundred?" I laugh again, and she moans. "When you do that, I can feel it all the way through my body."

"Then I shall plan on making you laugh quite often," I tell her, and I mean it. I move slowly over her again, and when I push into her this time, I'm acutely aware of how my spur taps against her clit, and the little tremor of response that tells me she's enjoying it.

Well, that and the bellow in my ear she just made, and the fact that she's grabbed one of my horns again.

Confident, I pump into her again and start a slow, steady rhythm, intending to make long, languid love to my human.

It doesn't work that way. Every time I thrust into her, she gasps and clenches, and I can feel the little spasms of pleasure deep in her cunt. She tightens around my cock each time, and the wet, gripping heat of her is impossible to tune out. I can't find a rhythm after all. Instead, I make each thrust as good as I can possibly make it for both of us, watching her response each time. I can feel her tensing as I pound into her, and her little whimpers escalate until she's keening in my ear, her nails digging into the plates on my shoulders.

"Kiv," she breathes. "Kiv. Kiv."

"My sweet Fran," I tell her, pushing a tendril of sweaty hair off her brow. She's so lovely in her pleasure that I can't look away. "All mine."

"Yours," she promises, even as I thrust into her again. She makes a little choking sound, arching her hips, and with my next thrust, she comes again, shuddering and wrecked.

Now I can come, too. I pump into her, harder and faster, desperate to join her in her pleasure. She murmurs filthy promises in my ear even as her breasts bounce with every thrust, and it's enough to make me lose control. I grunt her name between gritted teeth as I spill deep inside her, pouring my essence into her body and claiming every bit of her.

Fran is mine. All mine.

I collapse against her, then roll on my side so I don't crush her under my weight, and flip her onto me. We're both sweaty and sticky from our lovemaking, but I like it. It definitely feels a little deviant, but why shouldn't I revel in such things? Nothing about our relationship would be by the law. No sense in starting now.

As I catch my breath, I caress Fran's face. "How are you, my sweet?"

She gives me a dreamy smile. "Better than good." She wiggles on top of me, wrinkling her nose. "Your spur's still pushing me in all the right places."

"Making you think of round two, then? Give a pirate a moment, won't you?"

Fran chuckles and lies down atop my chest, her arms around me and her cheek against my heart. "You can have a moment, then. But just one."

"You are the very soul of generosity, my love."

She smiles, but the look she gives me is curious. "So you were really going to take me back to Earth? Even though it's dangerous?" At my nod, she continues. "What about the other girls? The other human slaves you were going to rescue?"

I know what she's asking. She doesn't want to sacrifice their happiness for her own. "Don't get any ideas, my sweet. You're stuck with me. As for the other females, we can still rescue them, I suppose. Let them decide their own fates. They can take their chances here with us, or we can drop them off at a safe place that harbors humans...or we can take them back to Earth."

"What are the others going to think of that?" She looks worried. "Alyvos won't like it."

"Alyvos gripes about everything, but he's also the first to sign up for a dangerous job. He's a good man. He'll go along with it." I pat her arm. "And who knows, perhaps we can find him a human friend. Or perhaps my brother might like some extra help on his farm."

The smile she gives me is everything. "It sounds like a wonderful plan."

It rather does. "Been meaning to visit my brother anyhow."

EPILOGUE

FRAN

Months Later

Chloe's not like how I pictured her. When Kivian told me that his brother had married a human and they were farmers on a distant agricultural planet, I pictured a tall, strapping blonde who could wrestle a goat and handle someone as big (and overbearing) as a mesakkah can be. The girl in front of me is dainty, dark-haired, and can't be much older than I am.

She's also incredibly excited to meet me. "Kivian didn't tell us he'd gotten married!" She envelops me in an octopus-like hug, all arms and squeezing. "I'm so excited to see you! It's been forever since I looked at another human face!"

"I'm excited to see you, too," I tell her, and I mean it. Not because she's human—we've been busy rescuing slaves between runs and I've actually seen several—but because she's my sister-in-law and she's pregnant with a half-mesakkah baby.

It's something Kivian and I have talked about. We're not ready to jump into a family just yet—mostly because there's no room aboard the already overcrowded *Fool* as it is. But we're thinking about it, and I want to pick Chloe's brain. "I brought you a care package. I hope that's all right."

Her eyes widen and she takes a step back, a hand to her mouth. "Earth food?"

I grimace. "Not quite. But I taste-tested everything in here and tried to find things that hit the right notes of sweet and sour. You know if it was up to Kiv, he'd just throw a bunch of those breakfast noodles in here and call it a day."

Chloe giggles and clasps her hands. "You're so thoughtful. Thank you!"

"It's on the ship. I'll go get it for you." I smile at her, trying not to stare at her tiny house. It looks a little like a human yurt, right down to the crude wall-hangings and almost-primitive kitchen. It's clean and tidy, but it's definitely a lot different from the ship.

"I'll come with you," Chloe says eagerly, and grabs my arm, linking hers through it.

I can't help but laugh at her enthusiasm. "You know, Kivian described you as shy and quiet."

She giggles again. "Did he? Maybe he needs to stay a bit longer and get to know me better. I don't think Jutari would use the same descriptions."

Which is funny, because as we head out of the house, we see the two brothers standing by one of the fields. Jutari gestures at the crops swaying in the light breeze on Risda III, while Kivian has his hands on his hips and stares outward. It's easy to tell who's who, in my eyes. They might have similar stances, but only one's wearing the finest, most ornate sleeves this side of the galaxy. My Kivian has a weak spot for nice clothing, even though he pretends it's all a show. I know him well enough to not give him too much shit for it, though.

I think it's kind of cute.

It's interesting to see the brothers standing side by side, though. They're the same shade of blue, relatively similar builds, but Jutari's heavier and more muscular, and his hair is longer. He's got more tattoos than my Kivian and he looks far more brutal and savage. He's actually a little frightening, whereas my Kivian gets by on his flirtiness and easygoing manner.

"Will you guys be staying long?" Chloe asks, interrupting my thoughts.

"A week at least, I think," I tell her. "Kiv wanted to help Jutari out with some supplies, and the rest of the crew's taking a break on the nearby station. It's just us for a few days and then we round everyone up for another run."

"A run?" she asks as we board the *Fool's* dock.

"It's better if you don't ask," I tell her lightly. "It can't get you into trouble later on."

Her eyes widen. "Piracy? Kivian hasn't turned over a new leaf since getting married?"

"Nope. I didn't ask him to. All I asked was for a gun so I could help out because I hate staying behind."

Chloe looks shocked. "You help out?"

I nod and lead her toward the cargo bay, then type in the passcode to unlock my personal stash, where I've kept her treats. I had to lock them up or Tarekh and his never-ending stomach would have demolished them before we ever made it here. "I enjoy it. Besides, it's kind of cool to think that no one ever suspects a human woman to be armed and dangerous."

It's actually made several of our jobs easier. I dress up in my "pet" costume and pack a few weapons away. It's helped out in many a pinch, and I have to admit I'm as addicted to the thrill of piracy as much as Kivian is. The post-robbery adrenaline-rush sex is *amazing*.

"Wow. I was...well, I was hoping you guys would stay a while. When I heard Kivian had a wife, I thought maybe you'd want to set up shop here on Risda. Buy a nearby farm." She gives me a hopeful look.

I move forward and pluck a box of trentii cookies off of one of my shelves. I knew she'd ask. Kivian asked me the same thing before we arrived here. Did I want to give up our life for something safer? Settle down like his brother did? Have a calm, peaceful life of crops and whatever passes for cattle out here?

But I love my pirate. I love his silly, flirty grins. I love his easygoing personality. I love how he'd just as soon rob a person as shake their hand. He's naughty and fun and has a secret side that loves rich fabric and ornate clothing and yet still manages to be utterly masculine and sexual. I love that he doesn't give a damn about what anyone thinks...except me.

I wouldn't change anything about him. "I married a pirate," I tell her simply. "I don't think this is the life for him."

And it's not the life for me, either. My life is with Kivian, at his side, being his partner in every way. We'll stay with Jutari and Chloe for a while, and then head back out, breaking laws and taking risks. We'll trick someone out of their money and steal a shipment to sell to someone else, and then we'll return to our rooms, play sticks with no clothes on, and make love until the dawn.

I wouldn't change a thing. Because now, I'm a pirate, too. I'm more than Kivian's pet human. I'm his wife and lover. I'm his partner.

And I'm beyond happy.

AUTHOR'S NOTE

Guys.

The last thing I need to write is another series. I've got Fireblood Dragons. I've got Ice Planet Barbarians. I'm starting up Icehome. I've got New York stuff I do (which is nothing like this stuff, but it still fits on the schedule).

But sometimes the brain wants what it wants, and my brain this time wanted to write Kivian's story. And while writing Kivian's story, I of course gave him a crew and...

hangs head

You know where this is going, right? Right.

Another series. DAMN IT, BRAIN.

I don't know what it'll be called yet. I don't know when book two will be coming out, but it'll probably be Alyvos or Tarekh, and it'll be another novella like this one (er, even though this one was almost a full length novel) and it'll happen when I need to squeeze in a release between much longer books.

So there you go. You didn't ask, but you shall receive. <3

In the meantime, I wasn't sure how much I would enjoy writing pirates. I mean...arr, matey. *shrug* But then Kivian showed up in my brain wearing fancy clothes and with a laughing smile and I was like, all right, this is my kind of pirate. Fran, naturally, likes to take him down a peg or two - my favorite kind of heroine - so they were a lot of fun to write. I hope you enjoyed them as well.

A couple of people have asked about the writing on the heroine's back on the cover. I thought about writing it in, but it didn't seem to 'fit' the story. I use a lot of stock photography and finding just the right feel for the cover for me is more important than getting the details 100% right. Which is why he's got a belt around her neck - because dayum, that's sexy. And why he's not as massive as he should be in the picture. Most cover models are not massive guys, and football players won't hold still for a photo. ;) So I hope you enjoy the cover anyhow! Let's just pretend she has some inspirational sort of quote on her back...or something filthy that she got tattooed while on a drunken bender at college and wants to forget about. Sure, we'll go with that.

Next up - ICEHOME. I swear it's coming. I've even had conversations with Kati Wilde (my cover artist) about what I want on the cover. She might be a little frightened. It's cool. I'm excited with the direction things are heading, and she knows I just love to test her Photoshop skills.

I can't wrap this book without a huge, enormous, throbbing (ha) THANK YOU for my editor, Aquila Editing. You are a marvel and always there for me. You have saved my bacon many a time, and this book is better because of you. Thank you, thank you, thank you. Now, never leave me. ;)

Love to all!

— Ruby

PRISON PLANET BARBARIAN

Curious about Jutari and Chloe? Check out PRISON PLANET BARBARIAN and read their story!

(Click on the graphic to borrow/buy!)

Being kidnapped by aliens is one thing.

Being kidnapped by aliens and sent to a prison planet is something infinitely worse.

Here in Haven's prison system, I'm stranded among strangers, enemies, and the most ruthless criminals in the galaxy. There's no safety for a human woman here, especially not one branded as a murderer. I'm doomed to a fate worse than death.

*Then -- he decides I should be **his**. His name's Jutari. He's seven feet tall, blue, and horned. He's an assassin and one of the most dangerous prisoners here. He's like no one I've ever met before...and he might be my only chance.*

This story stands completely alone and is only marginally connected to the Ice Planet Barbarians series. You do not need to read those books in order to follow this one.

ICE PLANET BARBARIANS

Need more big blue aliens? Does a brutal alpha male possessing his delicate human female make you as happy as it makes me? If you like that sort of thing, I'd love for you to give ICE PLANET BARBARIANS a try. It's the start of a long, on-going series that's very dear to my heart and also stars some very big blue aliens.

As always, my books are free to read in KU! Just click through the graphic to borrow/buy!

You'd think being abducted by aliens would be the worst thing that

could happen to me. And you'd be wrong. Because now, the aliens are having ship trouble, and they've left their cargo of human women - including me - on an ice planet.

And the only native inhabitant I've met? He's big, horned, blue, and really, really has a thing for me...

RUBY DIXON READING LIST

ICE PLANET BARBARIANS
Ice Planet Barbarians
Barbarian Alien
Barbarian Lover
Barbarian Mine
Ice Planet Holiday (novella)
Barbarian's Prize
Barbarian's Mate
Having the Barbarian's Baby (short story)
Ice Ice Babies (short story)
Barbarian's Touch
Calm(short story)
Barbarian's Taming
Aftershocks (short story)
Barbarian's Heart
Barbarian's Hope
Barbarian's Choice
Barbarian's Redemption
Barbarian's Lady
Barbarian's Rescue

Barbarian's Tease

FIREBLOOD DRAGONS
Fire In His Blood
Fire In His Kiss
Fire In His Embrace

BEDLAM BUTCHERS
Bedlam Butchers, Volumes 1-3: Off Limits, Packing Double,
Double Trouble
Bedlam Butchers, Volumes 4-6: Double Down, Double or
Nothing, Slow Ride
Double Dare You

BEAR BITES
Shift Out of Luck
Get Your Shift Together
Shift Just Got Real
Does A Bear Shift in the Woods
SHIFT: Five Complete Novellas

WANT MORE?

For more information about upcoming books in the Ice Planet Barbarians, Fireblood Dragons, or any other books by Ruby Dixon, 'like' me on Facebook or subscribe to my new release newsletter. If you want to chat about the books, why not also check out the Blue Barbarian Babes fan group?

Thanks for reading!

<3 Ruby

Printed in Great Britain
by Amazon

16699963R00098